Decemb

For Tom,

May everyone find pleasure in your ebullient disposition.

Vince Vawter

Jeremiah, My Servant

...Vincent J. Vanston

Copyright © 2004 by Vincent J. Vanston

All rights reserved. No part of this book shall be reproduced or transmitted in any form or by any means, electronic, mechanical, magnetic, photographic including photocopying, recording or by any information storage and retrieval system, without prior written permission of the publisher. No patent liability is assumed with respect to the use of the information contained herein. Although every precaution has been taken in the preparation of this book, the publisher and author assume no responsibility for errors or omissions. Neither is any liability assumed for damages resulting from the use of the information contained herein.

This is a work of fiction. Names, characters, places, and incidents either are the product of the author's imagination or are used fictitiously. Any resemblance to actual events or locales or persons, living or dead, is entirely coincidental.

ISBN 0-7414-2251-4

Published by:

INFINITY
PUBLISHING.COM

1094 New DeHaven Street, Suite 100
West Conshohocken, PA 19428-2713
Info@buybooksontheweb.com
www.buybooksontheweb.com
Toll-free (877) BUY BOOK
Local Phone (610) 941-9999
Fax (610) 941-9959

Printed in the United States of America

Printed on Recycled Paper

Published December 2004

Prologue

People call me Yahweh, Allah, Elohim, God, Jehovah, or Lord. I'm the creator and sustainer of all people and things. I wrote short stories, poetry, narrative, and allegory in my last work, the Bible, even letters, but this is my first novel. A novel is long, and some of my people have difficulty concentrating even on a short story like *Jonah*.

They prefer pithy sayings such as they find in Proverbs or Ecclesiastes. They even like parts of the Song of Songs because of the sexual overtones. But a novel? We'll see.

I have had servants everywhere in the world, great servants whom I loved and cherished. I love every person in the world, but there's a big difference between liking and loving.

I love everyone, but I don't like everyone. Jeremiah I like, just as much as I liked David. Some people are upset that I liked David. They admit he was my devoted servant, but they also know he was a scoundrel at times.

The day David brought up the Ark of the Covenant from the house of Obed-edom to the city of David, I couldn't believe my eyes. There was David, clad only in a linen apron, his backside sticking out, dancing before the sign of my presence with all his energy, shouting words of praise to me, and playing the trumpet. David was so human, a man after my own heart, wild and crazy in his love of me.

John the Baptist was one of the greatest men ever born, but I never liked him. He ranted at everyone to repent, raved like a mad man, screamed at the Pharisees, dressed like a hippie, and ate locusts, of all things. He was the best person to prepare the way for my Son, but I wouldn't want to spend an evening in his company. He's too intense. He still gives all of us up here a headache.

Some people do great work for me, but they aren't pleasant about it. Jerome was like John the Baptist. Jerome performed a herculean task in translating both the Old and New Testament writings into Latin from the Hebrew and Greek so the people of his day could understand them, but he had a crotchety disposition. When he argued with someone, like the monk Jovinian who wrote and preached the equality of the states of marriage and virginity, he was crude. He made my writings better known through his translations, but I never liked him, and to this day, I try to avoid him when I see him.

Jeremiah complains to me so much I block my ears. I have to admit he has a hard life with his wife, his daughter, and his sister-in-law. He hates being my servant, and he rues the day he was born. Just listen.

"Woe is me, my mother, that you ever bore me, a man of strife and contention to the whole land," Jeremiah said. "Why is my pain unceasing, my wound incurable, refusing to be healed? Truly, you are to me like a deceitful brook, like waters that fail."

"Jeremiah."

"Yes, Lord."

"Before I formed you in your mother's womb, I knew you, and before you were born I consecrated you. Now I appoint you as my prophet. You must speak as I tell you to speak."

"Ah, Lord God!" Jeremiah said. "Truly I do not know how to speak for I am only a boy. Choose someone else, Lord. I don't want to be your prophet for men have tortured your prophets and killed them."

"Do not say, 'I am only a boy.' You shall go to all to whom I send you, and you shall speak whatever I command you. Do not be afraid of anyone, for I am with you to deliver you."

"But Lord, I want to be an ordinary man, to have a wife and the blessings of children."

Then I put out my hand and touched his mouth. "Now I have put my words in your mouth. You will speak them whenever I command."

I allowed Jeremiah to have one child, but a child who was a burden for many years, rather than a blessing. He needed some earthly consolation and affection, however, so I gave him a grand-daughter, Naomi, to be his disciple. I did not anoint Jeremiah to bear witness against my peoples' infidelities, as I did Elijah, Elisha, Amos, Hosea, Micah, Zephaniah, Nathan, and most of the other prophets, but to bear the weight of their transgressions. I chose Jeremiah to be a suffering servant.

Why did I bring trouble on my servant Jeremiah? I have my own agenda. Now I'll begin the novel and see what the critics think of it. Maybe it will become a best seller like the Bible.

1.

Jeremiah knew he was a saint by the grace of God, and someday all the people in the township would acknowledge it, not to his own glory, but to the glory of the Lord. Before he died, the Lord told him he must ask the township supervisors to erect a memorial statue to commemorate his saintly life and to hold it up as an example for both old and young. He was seventy-nine years old, soon to be eighty, and time was running down. Most of the previous night he had lain awake, trying to decide when he would begin his final burden. Like all prophets he wished to delay the day of reckoning. At 6:30 A.M., he slipped out from under the covers and rolled himself onto his knees next to the bed and prayed.

"O Lord, you have enticed me, and I was enticed; you have overpowered me, and you have prevailed. I have become a laughingstock all day long; everyone mocks me." Jeremiah struck the sides of his head with his hands.

"And now you command me to persuade the township supervisors to erect a monument to me because of my good deeds! They'll put me away in a mental hospital, and after they lock me up, they'll beat me. Please, get someone else to be your servant."

Jeremiah rose from his knees, shaking his head in resignation. He knew his prayers were in vain.

Jeremiah was tall and so thin he looked like a monk who had been fasting forty years, and his beard and mustache made him look like the prophet he was. As long as anyone could remember, he wore three sweaters and a heavy plaid shirt in the winter because he claimed they were warmer than one heavy coat. He pulled each sweater over his head as if he were vesting for a religious ceremony at which he was going to be the celebrant. Once he was vested, he went downstairs.

As he walked into the kitchen, Sarah Kingsman Bowman, his wife; Anna, his daughter; and his granddaughter Naomi were having breakfast.

"If you go out in this cold, Jeremiah, the veins in your nose will freeze, your nose will turn grayish-blue and bulbous, and it will take three days for it to return to normal."

Sarah looked deep into the cup of tea she was sipping as if what she had said wasn't so important as concentrating on the rich taste of the tea which she drank all day.

Somewhere she had read that tea was anti-carcinogenic. None of the Kingsmans had ever had cancer, and she was determined not to be the first to disgrace the line.

Sarah never slouched over her breakfast like the rest of her small family. She sat up straight, her head and chin and shoulders drawn back as she had been taught to do when she had studied ballet with Miss Baxter.

"I'll be all right," he said, irritated she still talked to him like a child at his age and after fifty-two years of marriage. "I've been going out in Pennsylvania winters for seventy-nine years. I think I know how to dress for them."

"That God of yours must take special care of people who have no sense," she said, smiling faintly at the pleasure she derived from teasing him, but also taking aim at his God.

Her God had manners, restraint, civility, enough reserve to let everyone alone, and perhaps even enough good sense not to exist. Jeremiah's God was bristling and bustling, meddling in everyone's affairs, just like an old busybody, afraid that he would miss something.

"Hmph," was his only response. "Come on, Naomi," he said to his grand-daughter. "Finish your breakfast, and come with me. I'll put the stew in a container while I'm waiting for you."

"I made a pot of oatmeal. You eat some before you go, Jeremiah. You need some hot cereal that will cling to your bones on a freezing day like this," Sarah said. She watched over him and was upset when he didn't take care of his health for she couldn't imagine life without him.

"I can't eat today, Sarah. You know that. I'm fasting for the Rogers baby," he said.

"What good is your fasting going to do? The baby is too small to live. It'd be a blessing if the baby died. She probably has brain damage."

"Whether we live for the Lord or whether we die for the Lord, we're the Lord's, according to Paul. It's up to the Lord to say who lives and dies, not us," Jeremiah said.

"Then why don't you let him decide instead of pestering him all the time with your fasting and prayers. If he exists, I'm sure he has enough brains to make up his own mind," she said. "He doesn't need you bothering him all the time. You're probably a pain in his side."

"He says to keep pestering him all the time until he gets sick enough of all our prayers and gives us what we're asking for. It's right there in the Bible," he said, pointing to the ever present book.

"You try to fill everybody's mind with that nonsense of yours. If there is a God, he certainly isn't checking the daily hospital report on the Rogers baby."

"He knows each of his sheep by name," he said.

"Who in his right mind would want to be a sheep?" she said, lifting her arms in exasperation. "Now you eat some cereal and stop this nonsense."

"I'm going to fast for your sake tomorrow so the Lord won't take what you said seriously. I don't want him to get mad at you," Jeremiah said.

"I'm sure he's as unconcerned about me as he is about the Rogers baby. Do you think he listens in on every conversation in the world like some nosy old gossip?"

"Are you ready, Naomi?" he asked, weary of arguing with Sarah who was quicker and more articulate than he was.

Naomi looked at her mother for permission to go, but Anna never noticed what anyone said unless it was directed to her. She was a large woman, thick through the neck and shoulders and arms, and she ate such huge quantities of food that the act of eating required her complete concentration. Naomi was twelve years old and had long become accustomed to this, and so she took her mother's silence as permission or refusal depending on her desire to go somewhere or not.

"Where are we going?" she asked, finishing her milk and putting on her jacket and boots, eager to accompany him. She was her grandfather's disciple, listening to all his sayings and practicing good deeds with him. Everytime she had to hand in a paper for class and she could choose her own topic, she wrote about her grandfather.

Sarah looked at her grand-daughter with love, but without approval. She would have liked to form her and mold her, but Naomi was more fond of her grandfather. The only battles she won were the times when Jeremiah tried to keep the child home from school to go with him on some fool errand or other like clipping the grass around Leighton Jones' grave before Memorial day because Anna Jones was in the hospital and couldn't get there to do it herself.

Jeremiah filled Naomi with God and heaven and good deeds, belittling books and studies and education to the point where Sarah was certain Naomi would want to quit school when she turned sixteen.

Everytime Jeremiah saw Naomi studying, he used to say, "You're not supposed to spend life studying about life. You're supposed to spend life living it."

"She's got a fine mind," Sarah would say. "Let her use it. Anna never used hers."

And then Jeremiah Bowman would keep still, distraught that his only daughter, his only child, Anna, had, as an unmarried woman, become pregnant with Naomi, never married the boy, nor even wanted to marry him, nor told them who he was.

Once Anna had delivered herself of the child, she stayed at home, not to take care of Naomi, but to retire from the world. She felt she had been a disappointment to her parents.

In her own defense, however, she also knew she was the product of one of her mother's last eggs and her father's worn out sperm, not smart enough for her mother, not good enough for her father. And so she gave them what very few people in the world ever get, a second chance to raise a baby girl and see if they could get it right this time.

As Naomi grew older, Anna blended more and more into the kitchen table where she sat for two and three hours at a time, eating and eating, until some days she was able to connect all three meals without ever leaving the table except to relieve herself.

"It's a good thing we have a large plot of land," Sarah often said, sipping her tea and trying to control her revulsion over Anna's incessant chewing. Jeremiah planted potatoes, turnips, cabbages, and corn, Anna's favorites.

And they had apple and pear and peach trees which produced more fruit than they needed. Despite Anna's insatiable appetite, Jeremiah had enough fruit and vegetables to bring to his sick neighbors when he visited them. He blessed God for the great harvest he took in each year.

Jeremiah had only one animal, a cow, but she was a great milker. His two dogs, Spider and Simone, were supposed to be watchdogs, but they seemed more interested in sleeping than watching for intruders.

Naomi was so fascinated with her mother's capacity to eat that she spent one entire day writing down everything her mother had eaten: seventeen potatoes, four heads of cabbage, eleven turnips, and thirteen ears of corn. She handed in her statistics to her teacher for a report in Health and Hygiene class, but the teacher gave her a "D" because she said the report was supposed to be based on fact and not made up like a story.

"We won't be gone long," Jeremiah said. "This stew of mine is going to take a lot of the pain out of Mary Carroll's grieving."

"I don't see how your stew is going to heal the pain of losing Bill, but I hope it does," Sarah said. Her mind wandered to the days of her and Bill's intimacies. For the past few months she had been having trouble with her memory, just little things, but she had no trouble remembering the time she shared with Bill.

"Funny thing how Mary fell asleep like that and didn't even know he was dead until the next morning when she woke up," he said.

He had ladled all the stew into a plastic container and was putting the lid on and saying a silent prayer it would fit tight. Then he stretched four rubber bands from top to bottom to keep it from spilling. "When you're old, you need the warmth of two bodies more than when you're young. Doesn't make sense sleeping in twin beds."

Sarah sometimes wished he would not only sleep in another bed, but in another room because he tossed and turned at least two or three times a month as if he were wrestling with an angel of the Lord. After a night like that, she was exhausted the following day, while Jeremiah never showed any signs of weariness.

She loved having a man next to her in bed, however, and though their sex life at this age was reduced to five or six times a year, it was comforting to be held by a man and to know he found you desirable. Sarah was still a striking woman since age had treated her gently. Whenever she was restless and couldn't seem to sleep, he'd put his arm across her body and she'd fall asleep at once in the strength of his embrace.

"I'm ready, grandpa," Naomi said, looking at her mother for a last minute approval which never came.

"Put your wool hat on and pull it down over your ears," Sarah said to Jeremiah. "And wear that new red scarf I bought you. You're going to catch pneumonia, and I'm too old to nurse you back to health."

"Now don't start fussing over me," he said. "You know I don't go anywhere without my peaked cap, winter or summer, and I can't wear a scarf because I feel like I'm going to choke to death. Now just hush up about what I should or shouldn't wear. I won't be any burden on you."

"People as stubborn as you do dumb things that cause other people grief," Sarah said. "Don't get thick-headed like your Grandpa, Naomi. If you want to get anywhere in this life, you have to use your brains."

"Then maybe someday you'll grow up to become a school teacher like your Grandma," he said, believing her education had led her to be irreligious. He looked at Sarah, but she was sipping her tea, back straight, shoulders back, head high, eyes down. Despite her disapproval of his religious fervor, he knew she had blessed his life, and though his body was not up to it, he loved her with a smoldering passion.

Jeremiah bent his slender frame over Sarah and kissed her on the left cheek, and she reached up with her hand and patted him on his right cheek. Then he turned to Anna and kissed her. He was not assured by the Lord what the day would bring, and so he never left the house without kissing them goodbye.

Yahweh's Interlude

Sarah's O.K. She doesn't mean any harm, but when she tries to put manners on me and make me into a gentlemanly God, it turns me sour. Of course I'm a busybody, snooping into everyone's private life. If I wasn't nosy about how all my people were doing, what kind of God would I be?

She paid too much attention to that father of hers. He was intrigued with manners, a real prig, and thought learning and the worship of letters were all that anyone needed to live a good life. He was a gentleman all right, looking down at lesser mortals, setting himself above the plebians.

I hate to use this vulgar expresson, but he farted higher than his ass. I wish the old man were alive on earth to see what was going to happen in the next chapter. He'd be so embarrassed by Jeremiah that he'd never come out of his house.

Jonathan still struts around up here like most school teachers who think they know everything. Teachers are insufferable, but, thank goodness, they keep pretty much to themselves. They ignore me, and I ignore them, and that way we get along fine. They spend most of their time reading poetry to one another. Forgive the pun, but they really are the "Dead Poets Society."

I want you to pray that I'll keep my sanity. All these so called "canonized" saints are like prima donna's, and they drive me to distraction. These men and women sanctioned by some pope or other strut about as if they're better than everyone else.

The other day I heard James of Jerusalem say to one old guy and his wife, "You may have wheedled your way in here, but you're not the real thing. There are only a select few of us who've been "declared" saints."

I told James never to say that again to anyone or I'd

give him a thousand year mission to earth to count the Sunday collection at St. Patrick's Cathedral. The way these "saints" talk you'd think they came here with an unlimited warranty, while the rest of the people have a built in obsolescence. Next thing you know, they'll be checking on my credentials.

2.

Naomi had to skip every so many feet to keep up with her grandfather who had long legs and walked with huge strides. As heavily laden with flesh as Anna was, Naomi was as slender as her grandfather. She was fair, and she had blue eyes and blonde hair which led her grandparents to suspect her father might be Danish or German, but Anna never said who he was or what he was, so it was only conjecture.

Anna had been a sixth year student at college when she became pregnant. Sarah had insisted on her graduating from college, so she went every year and passed some courses, but never enough to graduate. She had neither the ambition nor the desire to get her degree, but college wasn't a bad life, so she returned every year until she became so upset with a course in Spanish, which was a language requirement and which she was taking for the third time, that she decided to get pregnant, have a girl-child, and let her parents start all over again.

On a cold February night she offered the warmth of her body to a student hungry for sex. She picked him because she heard he was very intelligent, and she wanted her daughter to be intelligent. Shutting her eyes and gritting her teeth as this stranger plowed away at her, she conceived on her first attempt.

When he approached her again in a maelstrom of lust, she looked at him as if she was puzzled he didn't know she had used him, shook her head in disbelief, turned, and walked away. She announced the news to her mother and father, and they allowed her to leave college and come home. Anna was relieved her terrible encounters with both education and sex were over.

Since Naomi was smart and attractive, she more than justified Anna's fall from grace. Anna's life's work had been finished by the age of twenty-five, and she had spent the last twelve years with feelings of accomplishment and peace.

Naomi was amazed that her grandfather was able to walk so fast and never had to breathe through his mouth. Everyone she knew, even the other kids at her school, had to breathe through their mouths when they walked fast in the cold weather. But her grandfather was so extraordinary that she had come to expect him to be different from everyone else.

"Grandma told me her father didn't want her to marry you. Is that right?" Naomi asked.

"True as the sun," he said. "She was a real determined lady, believe me, and she wasn't going to let her father tell her who she could marry. She was respectful to him because there was never a lady that loved her father as much as your Grandma, but she was full of grit when he tried to change her mind."

"Does my mother love you as much as Grandma loved her father?"

Most often Jeremiah Bowman had an answer for each of life's questions, but his daughter was a question he couldn't answer. She was hiding in a gravitational pull deep within herself that was too powerful for him to overcome, even though he fasted and prayed every day for her to rise to life again. He thought of Lazarus, and hoped Anna might come forth from the tomb of her mind, but nothing had changed since the day Naomi was born.

That his prayers were never answered was a stumbling block that challenged his faith, but he clung to the promise of the Lord that his prayers would be answered if he didn't give up. He assailed heaven each and every day, refusing to surrender to the sin of despair.

Before Anna finished high school, he realized he could not reach her, although he tried mightily, taking her on walks, playing games with her, talking to her. As he meditated on the life of Christ, trying to see where their paths crossed, he realized Christ had never been able to reach Judas, never been able to rescue him.

It was a poor analogy since Anna would not even give a thought to betraying Jeremiah, but some psychological problems such as Anna had defied any spiritual solution. Even the apostles were unable to cast out some demons because of their lack of faith. Maybe he lacked sufficient faith to save Anna from her demons.

"I think in her way your mother loves us both, Naomi, you and me. I just don't think she's able to show her love, and I feel bad about that."

"I do too," Naomi said, and she felt tears coming to her eyes.

"I know you do."

"But I have you, grandpa, and that makes up for a whole lot. You love me, don't you?"

"If you held out your arms as far as they could go, you'd still never be able to hold all my love for you. It's bigger than all the mountains in the state of Colorado," he said.

She felt the warm embrace of his love.

"Naomi," Jeremiah said, "we have to learn to do good while we still have time, especially for those who believe the same things as we do. That's one of the things Paul says." He found himself at a slight loss while he was talking because he liked to use his hands, but he was carrying the stew, and he was afraid he might fall and spill it.

"Now Catholics, like the Carrolls for instance, aren't the same as we are. They're Christians like we are, but they have a lot of queer ways about them." He nodded his head as if he had come to an agreement with himself. "Except for their statues. Now that's an idea I like."

Naomi tried to keep up with her grandfather and look at him while he was speaking because she didn't want to miss anything he said. The stories she wrote for class assignments about her grandfather made the other girls at school snicker, and they began to think she was crazy like her grandfather. But Naomi forgave them for not knowing any better. She had great things in mind for her future, and that was more than any of those silly girls could say.

She collected her grandfather's stories and sayings and wrote them down in small notebooks. She had written pages and pages about him, the things he said and the things he did. Jeremiah told her she was his Matthew, Mark, Luke, and John.

"You see, Naomi, if a person leads a good life and even better, a holy life, there ought to be a remembrance of that person in a statue or at the very least a monument. If a man writes a good book, people publish it for everyone to read. If a man paints a good painting, they hang it in a gallery for everyone to see. If a man sings a good song, they record it and play it on the radio for everyone to hear."

Now that his premises were solid, Jeremiah knew that his conclusion would be logical. "And so if a man leads a good life, they ought to make him a saint and cast his likeness in bronze, or at least alabaster.

"The only problem," and he knew it was a problem because even he couldn't think of a solution to it, "is that none of the Protestant religions 'makes' saints like the Catholics do, and so if you're a saint and a Protestant, no one will ever know about it except you and God, and that's no good because other people won't be inspired to read about your life and imitate your good deeds."

"Why don't you become a Catholic then? Maybe they'll make you a saint."

"Well, I wouldn't be much of a saint if I flip-flopped from believing in one thing to believing in something else now, would I? I could never believe the Pope is infallible, nor could I believe it's right to baptize a baby when other people, not the child, say she believes.

"The Popes make most of their saints out of priests

and nuns or somebody who lived life as a virgin. They cast a dead eye on you if they know you've had sex, so I don't think they'd give a married man like me the flicker of an eye. Besides, we're Americans, and they make hardly any American saints."

"I want to get married, Grandpa," Naomi said. She had a crush on Samuel Larson and thought she'd like to marry him, but she didn't know anything about love between a boy and a girl. "What's love like, Grandpa?"

"Well, if you feel yourself wanting to be with Sam a lot and you like to touch each other all the time, that's like love. It kind of leads up to the way you can have a baby, so you got to be thinking of the Lord too when you're out with Sam so you don't get carried away by all that touching."

"Is that how my mother got me?" Naomi asked.

"Just that very way," Jeremiah said.

"And she wasn't married?"

"No."

"Why did she do it then?"

"I don't know. I guess she wanted to give your grandmother and me a little girl to love."

"Do you love me, grandpa, even though my mother wasn't married, and what she did was a sin and all?"

Jeremiah had often thought of the wonderful fruits of his daughter's sin. Although he disapproved of what Anna had done, he didn't know how he had managed to live for sixty-seven years without Naomi.

His close world was filled with women: Sarah, Anna, his sister-in-law, Millicent, and Naomi, and he believed the three oldest loved him, even Millicent, in her own way. With Naomi, however, he could smell and touch her love. It was like a warm blanket on a cold night.

Jeremiah almost never read anything but the bible, but when Naomi was a baby, he read books to her, and she would listen to him as if the world around her had evaporated. She looked at him in adoration when he read, her blue eyes fixed on his mouth, and her imagination fascinated by the story of Big Bird, or Yertle the Turtle, or as she grew older, books like *The Lion, the Witch, and the Wardrobe*; *The Hobbit*; *Little Women*; *Alice in Wonderland* and others that she loved having him read and reread.

All those years before Naomi burst in on his life, he had tried to love and help people, imitating Christ in his care of the poor and afflicted. If Naomi was some sort of reward for the few good things he had done, Jeremiah thought the Lord had spoiled him by turning on a spigot of joy.

Each day Jeremiah offered a prayer in thanksgiving that Naomi was his grand-daughter. To be loved by Naomi was something special, undeserved, unmerited, like the grace of God. It was like those grape pickers in Matthew's gospel, where the last to begin work got just as much as the first, not fair in the eyes of the early morning pickers, but the kind gift of the owner of the vineyard. He would always cherish Anna for the gift of Naomi. If what she did was a sin, and he knew it was, it was a fine sin.

"Before you came, Naomi, there were some dark days in my life. Then there was you, breathtaking like the rising of the sun over the horizon. You know, Naomi, when somebody loves you as much as you love me and I love you, then you never feel alone, and you never feel sad, and you never lose hope because you know if even one person loves you that much, then everything will be fine."

Naomi would have taken his hand and held it forever, but Jeremiah had both hands on the pot of stew and she had to be content with just feeling like Cinderella must have felt when the prince found her.

Sometimes she had bad dreams about her grandfather's dying, and they were so vivid that she snuck out of bed, tiptoed to his room, peeked in, and watched the blankets move up and down with his breathing. The dreams made her sad because she knew he was old, and someday, soon maybe, he'd have to leave her.

When she was feeling real bad about this, she hoped she'd die first, and then he'd come to her, and they'd be together forever. If she lived to be an old woman, he might not even know her when she died and got to see him again. It wouldn't be much of a heaven if he didn't remember her.

"Grandpa, you've done more nice things for all kinds of different people than anyone I know. Why just yesterday it took us three hours to get that water line unfrozen for Widow Swartz, and she's Jewish and all."

The day was cold, and there was a wind chill that sent the thermometer to five below zero. The wind was whipping up the snow and hurling it at them. It stung their faces and they squinted to lessen the chance of getting lashed in their eyes.

It was a three mile walk to the Carroll's place, and although the snow wasn't deep, it was packed so hard it was slippery, and they had to watch each step. It was even colder than when they started out.

Jeremiah knew he should have worn his scarf and a different hat like Sarah said, but he'd always dressed this way, and he couldn't change now. He'd just endure the cold because it was God's cold, and cold somehow made the world a purer place.

"Now every saint has to have a disciple, someone who follows in his footsteps and carries on his good works when he dies," he said. "You're my disciple, Naomi, and it'll be up to you to carry on my work.

"You're kind of like Sancho who rode along with Don Quixote. The only problem is that you have to walk since those doctors won't let me drive anymore, and we don't have a horse or even a mule."

"I don't mind, grandpa. Our teacher said being outdoors and walking is good for you. Besides, you told me neither Jesus nor Paul had a car."

"That's right. They walked everywhere they went, except when they went by boat or on a donkey."

Jeremiah talked to Naomi as if she were grown up and knew all the things he knew, and since she didn't know a whole lot about the Bible, she had set herself to reading the passages he quoted from and tried to learn them by heart, especially chapter 25, verses 35 and 36 of Matthew's gospel.

Naomi thought about them all the time when she was with her grandfather. "..for I was hungry and you gave me food; I was thirsty and you gave me something to drink; I was a stranger and you welcomed me; I was naked and you gave me clothing. I was sick and you took care of me; I was in prison and you visited me."

Her grandfather was forever bringing food and drink and clothes to anyone who needed them, and she had seen him sit with sick people in their homes or the hospital and feed them or help them bathe. The only reason he stopped visiting inmates in prison was that he couldn't drive anymore and the prison was too far, even for him, to walk to.

"Now when we go inside, Naomi," Jeremiah said when they could see the Carroll's place, "they'll have a prayer kneeler in front of the casket. You know we don't go in for kneeling in church, but Catholics are crazy about kneeling. They'd almost rather kneel in church than sit, although some of them brace their butt on the pew instead of kneeling up straight. Just to be polite, we'll kneel down, and bow our heads in prayer for the soul of Bill Carroll."

Before Jeremiah could take another step, he began to twist and turn, trying valiantly to hold on to the pot of stew which was swirling, about to spill over. "Naomi," he cried, "take the pot before I drop it."

"What's the matter?" Naomi asked, taking the stew. "What's happening to you?" She was terrified.

"It's the Lord," Jeremiah said. "He's after me. Don't be afraid. He's wrestling with me."

Jeremiah fell to the ground. writhing and thrashing as if he were in a seizure. "No, I won't do it," he said. He was on his back, and he put out his hands in front of him as if he were pushing someone away. "No, let me alone," he cried.

But the Spirit wouldn't let him be. His body stiffened, and his head, back, and legs bounced on the hard pack of snow and ice. Then Jeremiah's eyes rolled up in his head, and he began to drool from the side of his mouth.

Naomi put the stew on the ground, bent down in the frozen snow and hugged him, stretching herself over him, trying to stop whatever was torturing him. "Grandpa, it's me, Naomi. I'm going to hug that evil spirit out of you." She squeezed tighter, trying to get her arms underneath him as far as she could.

His hands began to flail and his legs became spastic, and his frantic movements knocked Naomi off him. "Don't ask me to do that," Jeremiah shouted. Then Naomi heard a voice from the heavens.

"If you have raced with foot-runners and they have wearied you, how will you compete with horses? Arise, Jeremiah, and do my will. Open your mouth and proclaim my words, and do what I have commanded you. This is your lot, the portion I have measured out to you."

"I am your servant, Oh, Lord. I will do as you command, but you're not being fair. They'll mock me and persecute me and chase me from their home. I'll be ridden with disease in the eyes of this people."

"Jeremiah, if you don't follow my commands, I will pursue you every moment of the day. Whether you think my ways are fair or not is to me like a thought of the wind."

Jeremiah began to seize again, and again Naomi threw herself on him, exerting her will against the will of the voice she heard. But she was flung off him once again, sliding along the ice-slicked snow.

"All right, Lord. Let the child be. I will do as you have commanded me." When he had said this, his tremors ceased, and he sat up.

"Are you all right?" Naomi asked, bruised from the force of the sliding and still trembling in fear. "What happened to you? Who was speaking to you? What do you have to do to satisfy the spirit that seized you?"

"I have to perform a miracle," Jeremiah said, shaking his head in disbelief.

"What miracle?"

"I have to raise Bill Carroll from the dead." He could not believe the words he had spoken. "You saw what happened to me. It was the Lord. He ordered me to raise him up."

As he thought of what had happened, he began to shake his head in disbelief. This wasn't like in the time of Jesus when they just wrapped a body in linens and spices and laid it in a tomb. These were the days of embalming, of draining all the blood out of a person's body, of using a trocar to aspirate the contents of the cavities. Every vital organ was penetrated, then filled with embalming chemicals. There was no blood left to circulate. Raising someone from the dead in 1979 was impossible.

"I have no choice," Jeremiah said as he struggled to his feet. He was almost begging her for forgiveness. "I have no choice."

"But Grandpa, how are you going to do it? I've never seen you raise anyone from the dead." Naomi was afraid and she began to shiver, but if she could live through this, there'd be a story to tell that she heard before anyone else. She could see herself telling it over and over until she was an old woman like her grandmother.

"I don't know, but while I was in the trance, the Lord said to me, 'For you shall go to all to whom I send you, and you shall speak whatever I command you. Do not be afraid, for I am with you to deliver you.'"

Jeremiah was filled with fear. "I just don't know, Naomi. I have to trust the Lord. These Catholics are not going to like it when a Protestant performs a miracle, and on one of them!"

"We didn't spill the stew, grandpa, and it didn't get knocked over when you were whirling around on the ground," Naomi said, trying to comfort him, not knowing what else to say. "I bet they'll love the stew even if they don't love the miracle."

Jeremiah picked up the pot and trudged on until they came to the corpse house. It was a two storied house, and it looked like every other house on the block. Bill had not made a lot of money in his teaching career, but he had raised all his children in this house and fit them in somehow.

Naomi opened the gate, and walked directly in back of her grandfather as if she didn't want anyone to see her. Someday she hoped she would have his confidence and be able to walk right into groups of adults like she was the Lord's own messenger, but she was shy with strangers.

Last year Jeremiah had taken her to see Sister Rachel preach at the high school football stadium, and when Naomi saw her, all in white, preaching about Jesus to those thousands of people, everyone more quiet than you could imagine, at that moment she realized what she wanted to do with her life.

She was going to have sex and babies and watch over them, and they'd have a mother like she never had, but that would be only a part of her life. Preaching like Sister Rachel, preaching the words of her grandfather for as long as she lived, that was what she wanted to do more than anything.

"Seeing Sister Rachel was a calling, a clear sign," her grandfather had said. "You've been anointed, Naomi. You've been chosen."

She knew she was going to be a vessel of clay, filled to the brim with the Lord. He would work mighty deeds through her like He was going to do this very morning through her grandfather.

"Good morning, Mrs. Lally, and George, how're you

feeling? Over that touch of the gout, are you? Mrs. Fitzsimmons, you're starting to look yourself again. Take care she doesn't overdo it, Jim."

And this was the way the greetings went as Jeremiah made his way to the kitchen with the stew. He knew everything about each one of them, even though they were Catholics, and he knew their children and grandchildren.

He knew each woman's maiden name and her father, mother, brothers, and sisters. He knew when they were ailing and when times were bad, and he knew all these things because he made it his business to know them. And he helped them all whenever they were in need unless they wouldn't accept his help.

"A saint's of this world, not the next until he's dead, so he ought to concern himself about what's going on here," Jeremiah had said to Naomi, repeating some of his sayings several times when she was writing them down so people would have an exact record.

Naomi carried a small pad with her to take notes. They stirred her memory when she made the entries in her diary before she went to sleep each night. Long before she started preaching on her own, she would write the gospel according to her grandfather.

After they had given the stew to the women in the kitchen, they made their way to the grieving widow, Mary Carroll, who was sitting in an easy chair at the head of the casket, a handkerchief to her red nose, and tears running down her wrinkled face in great rivulets. Her hair was parted in the middle and pulled back severely to where she had fastened it in a tight knob at the back of her head. She looked more unattractive than usual, a stubby woman with surplus flesh.

"Cry tears of joy, Mary," Jeremiah said, bending over and patting her hand gently. "He's in heaven, the Lord knows. Dying in your sleep is a blessed death."

"Who's that behind you?" Mary asked, ignoring his

words of sympathy and peering behind him.

"This is Naomi," he said, reaching for her to come out from behind him and offer her sympathy. "You know my grand-daughter."

"I'm sorry about Mr. Carroll," Naomi said, curtsying, not knowing what to do and being mad at herself for not having asked her grandfather.

"Thank holy Jesus your wife had respect enough not to come," Mary Carroll said, ignoring both Naomi's awkwardness and her expression of sorrow. "They were sleeping with one another before we got married. You knew that, didn't you?"

"Now, Mary, that was over fifty years ago, before I even knew Sarah. It's long over and done with. In his own prayer, Jesus says we'll only get forgiveness from him in the same measure as we forgive others."

"I won't forgive her, not even now. I think Bill compared me to her all the time. It wasn't fair," Mary said.

Jeremiah Bowman began to warm up for a sermon, and as he did, his voice grew loud. "What makes a Christian different from other people is that he takes the Sermon on the Mount as his guide. He believes in mercy and meekness and love. Luke tells us in his gospel to love our enemies."

Naomi stared hard at the corpse of William Carroll, a thing which she had resolved not to do, but which was the only thing that kept her from crying as everyone in the living room and the kitchen began crowding toward the casket, fascinated, yet appalled by the preaching of old Jeremiah.

It was early in the morning, but there was a large number of people gathered to offer Mary comfort. Some were there for the food, and some for the drink to ward off the cold day, but they also felt bad about poor Bill.

No one will ever believe me when I tell them I knew what was going to happen, Naomi thought to herself, trying to prop up her nerves, while wishing at the same time she could disappear.

"....now if there's one little thing we hold against our brother or sister, then we cannot approach the altar of the Lord with our gift," Jeremiah continued, gesturing expansively now that his hands were free of the stew.

"Get out of my house!" Mary Carroll began screaming. "Get out of my house, Jeremiah!" Mary couldn't stand it any longer, this self appointed preacher babbling pious nonsense over the body of her husband who had slept with Sarah before Jeremiah, and him telling everyone to forgive the both of them. What kind of man was he anyway?

"What did I do wrong, Mary? Why are you so angry?" he asked, confused as always when he was told to stop doing good. "I'm only trying to honor the memory of your dear husband."

"You don't know how to act proper in a Catholic corpse house," she shouted at him, releasing the tears again and somehow managing to contract her features so she looked more homely than she did on an ordinary day. "You're so disrespectful to us Catholics that you wouldn't even settle yourself on the prayer kneeler for a second. And for your information, only our priest is allowed to preach to us, not some handyman."

"Didn't I tell you about the kneeler, Naomi, before we even came in here to pay our respects?" he asked, irritated with himself. "I guess I'm getting forgetful, Mary," he said to her, trying to hold her hand which she kept pulling away from him until it looked as if their tug-of-war would become more important than anything they had to say.

Finally, Mary gave in and let him hold her hand so she might be well rid of him. "Forgive me, Mary, I meant only good." Then he turned to the casket, knelt on the kneeler, and spoke to the body of Bill Carroll. "Rest in peace, William. You were a good father and a good man."

"And a good Catholic," Mary hissed at him.

Jeremiah didn't answer her. He stood up, stepped to the left of the kneeler, and stretched out his hand to touch the forehead of Bill Carroll. Before anyone could tell him to take his hands off the body, he said in a loud voice so that he could be heard throughout the house, even into the kitchen, "In the name of Jesus the Lord, I say to you, arise."

Everyone was struck dumb. No one could believe what Jeremiah had said. Mary's two oldest sons shouted, "you Protestant bastard, get out of here or we'll throw you out!" Kevin and Conor Carroll grabbed his arms and pulled them up behind his back, and started to drag him away.

"Let my grandfather alone, you bullies," Naomi shouted at them, punching them with her small fists. "You're hurting him. Stop it."

Mary Carroll screamed, a piercing scream of terror and fright and dread. Her sons let go of Jeremiah and turned toward their mother. Then everyone saw what Mary had seen.

Bill Carroll was sitting up in the casket, stretching his arms and nodding his head up and down, massaging the muscles of his neck as though he had been in an uncomfortable position. He began to rotate his head to shake off a profound headache. Out of the corner of his eye, he noticed there were people in the room, and so he swung his legs over what he thought was his couch, embarrassed that he had fallen asleep in front of company.

Because the casket rested on a bier which was only two feet wide, the weight of Bill Carroll tipped the casket over, and before anyone could rouse himself from awe and disbelief, he tumbled out of the casket. The kneeler broke his fall as his stomach caught on its prayer railing, but the lid of the casket caught him in the back of his neck and he howled with pain.

John Murphy, the undertaker, was distraught. He rushed forward to make sure no one damaged the casket while they were trying to get it off Bill Carroll, and as he motioned his hand like some army platoon leader, two of his men ran to his assistance. Together they lifted the casket and set it back on the bier, and they closed the lid so that it would suffer no further damage.

John Murphy had been the most successful funeral director in the township since he had gone into business fifty years ago. As he told everyone he met, "If you're not buried by John Murphy, there's a good chance you've not been buried at all."

Murphy drew his clientele, as he liked to call them, from not only the town of Carbon, a small, one-main-street town in the middle of the township, but from all the surrounding areas, Elk Mountain, Crystal Lake, Vandling, Fell, and the entire farming community surrounding Carbon.

He made sure to stop in every bar in the area at least once a week to buy the patrons drinks. He himself, however, treated his business as a holy mandate, and he would not indulge in drink lest his reputation suffer the least stain of impropriety. In his less generous moments, he entertained the thought the more people abused alcohol and tobacco, the sooner they would end up in one of his caskets.

His one flaw, if one can call it that, was that he loved money, and the more funerals he had, the more he could watch his money grow. Yet no one took him for a miser except his wife who longed for a vacation now and then, something he frowned on.

"Suppose someone dies and I'm on vacation," he would say to her. "How would that look? Wouldn't they remind me for the rest of my days that I wasn't here when their mother or father or husband or wife died? I'd be ashamed every time I ran into them."

He would spend money on drinks for the boys, on fine scotch for the priests in the surrounding parishes, on calendars for the Protestant churches, on aprons and cooking utensils for church suppers and carnivals, (items, of course, which bore the name of his funeral home), on generous donations to the volunteer fire department, and other civic endeavors, but what people did not realize was that all these costs were included in the price of their funerals. Whoever was a recipient of his generosity would pay for it on the day of his or her death. It would be part of an item on the bill titled "professional services." There was, however, nothing unethical in that.

For the first time in his many years in business, John Murphy could not control a situation. The pandemonium and chaos grew into hysteria and madness. People were fainting or rushing to get away from the resurrected Bill Carroll, or shouting praise for the wonders of the Lord, or crying and falling on their knees in prayer, or terrified by the miracle they were witnessing.

John Murphy had leaned against the wall behind the casket, and gradually let his body slide down until he was sitting on the floor. He held his head in his hands, trying to put pressure on his temples so his mounting headache would not turn into a stroke.

Since no one could see him, he allowed tears to come to his eyes as he thought of the money he had lost on this funeral, thousands of dollars which he had seen as another layer in his large cache. What could he charge Mary for? Not for the casket. Not for the concrete vault. Not for the hearse or the limousine and least of all for the embalming.

Sometimes people would remark to him about their fear of being buried alive, and he assured them such fear was unfounded if a person was embalmed since there would be no blood left to sustain them. Now what would he say to them? People would scoff at all of the patented answers he had developed through the years. "How do you know? Look at what happened to Bill Carroll," they would say in a tone of mockery.

As he began to think even more deeply, he realized this could ruin his reputation. It could make him a pariah among not only other undertakers, but among his own people. Hatred of Jeremiah filled his heart, and he damned the miracle worker. Nothing good could come of any of this.

Bill was confused, wondering why so many people were in his house, and why of all things, he had been inside a casket. He rubbed his neck which was sore from the casket lid hitting him, but otherwise he felt fine.

"Mary, what are all these people doing in our house?" he asked.

But Mary didn't answer him because she couldn't speak. She looked at him, and then she fainted, collapsing on the floor, making almost as much clamor as the casket when it tumbled over onto poor Bill.

Her sons Kevin and Conor tried to lift her from the floor, but her flesh spread all over her body like a shapeless mass, and they couldn't get a grip on her. Each time they tried to lift, her flesh kept sliding away from them, creating another amorphous mass. She had, as it were, no handles on her body to grasp. Some wise woman brought a pillow, and they lay it under her head and let her stay on the floor.

"Come on, grandpa, we have to get out of here," Naomi said, once the Carroll boys had let him go. "These Catholics are going to hurt you if we don't go." Jeremiah, himself awestruck by the power of the Lord that had been worked through him, let Naomi lead him out the door and away from the house.

He felt as if he were in a trance, gripped in a vise by the Spirit which was swirling through his body, his mind lifted on high. And he was exhausted, stumbling over the hard packed ground, slipping at times on the ice. If Naomi had not been holding him, he would have collapsed.

Naomi looked back toward the house and could see a number of people running after them, hurling snow and some loose ice at them. "Get away from here, you dirty Protestants," they shouted. But they didn't chase them far because they had rushed out of the house in a frenzy and had no coats on, and they would have frozen in the wind and ice and snow if they tried to pursue them. They shook their fists at them, but they went back into the warmth of the house and the newly resurrected Bill.

Once the shock left them and their belief restored them, they would have reason to party through the night And the stories they would tell, and how they would be envied by their family and friends who hadn't been there, and how they would express mock sympathy for those who had not seen Bill rise from the dead. "It's a pity you had more important things to do that day," they would say.

And there would be twenty or thirty different versions of what had happened, but no one would be able to say it was an illusion as much as they might like to because "that Protestant bastard" had performed the miracle before their eyes. Bill Carroll was living testimony of that, and John Murphy could give scientific testimony that he had been embalmed with the Dodge Company's best chemicals.

When Mary regained consciousness in her house of celebration and saw her husband who was trying to help her from the floor along with their sons, she uttered a sigh of dismay.

She had lost the money from the $100,000.00 insurance policy she had forced Bill to carry even through times when they could have used the monthly premium for necessities. And worse, it was a term insurance policy which was due to run out in two months. All those premiums for nothing. Jeremiah had wronged her just like his wife Sarah had wronged her.

When Naomi realized the crowd would not pursue them, she stopped for a moment so Jeremiah could regain his balance. Naomi began to tremble and shake. Now that she had saved her grandfather by getting him out of the house, she couldn't control herself.

"Why did the Lord tell you to work that miracle, Grandpa?" She began to cry. "He could have gotten us killed. What's the matter with Him? I thought you were his friend. Friends don't do things like that to friends. Why did He make you raise Bill Carroll up? Why didn't he let you raise up one of our own kind."

Jeremiah hugged Naomi until she began to calm down. He felt better now that the Spirit had let loose of him. Jeremiah held her hand and began to walk briskly, taking several deep breaths of frigid air, and the way it chilled his lungs gave him a sense of being alive in his world.

"Now, Naomi, don't fret. I know it was scary for you, and it was for me too. But don't get mad at the Lord." Jeremiah bowed his head and went into his deep thinking, and so Naomi bowed her head too. After a minute or two, Jeremiah raised his head and so did Naomi.

"The Lord told me why I had to do these things at Bill Carroll's wake." Jeremiah nodded his head in assent to the Lord's reasons. "First of all, He said to me, in order to have the township declare me a saint, I have to perform at least two miracles while I'm living.

"With Catholics, people have to go before a tribunal and give proof positive testimony with medical evidence that a miracle has taken place through the intercession of the dead person with God.

"But with me, the Lord said, there's no one who's going to take up my cause for canonization after I've died: first because it's an expensive process, and second because Protestants don't do things like that. So, what He decided was, that I'd have to perform the miracles while I was still alive."

"But why for Catholics? All they did was get so mad they tried to kill you." Naomi felt that if something happened to her grandfather, she'd be alone in her life, and she was too young to be alone. She felt safe with him as if she were in the hands of the Lord himself.

"Oh, Naomi, I was never worried about them killing me because the Lord isn't finished with me, and no one can harm me until He's completed his work in me. But doesn't it make good sense to show his power on my behalf in front of all those Catholics?

"Yep, they're the best kind of witnesses. If the Lord had told me to do it for some Protestant, the Catholics would never have believed it. Now, they have no choice. They're eyewitnesses." Jeremiah lowered his head in thought, and after a few moments, Naomi could see out of the side of her eye that he was ready to speak. "You know what bothers me most about all this, Naomi?"

"What grandpa?" Naomi asked.

"I'll never get that pot back we took the stew in, and your grandma Sarah will be mad as she can be." He laughed and squeezed Naomi's hand, and they walked homewards, thinking their own thoughts about the mighty deeds of the Lord.

Elohim's Interlude

This miracle was the best I ever performed through one of my servants! No blood left in the body. Every organ punctured and drained. Formaldehyde was the only liquid in his tissues and the main component of his body.

They could spread rumors about my son's resurrection from the dead, how the apostles came to the tomb at night and stole his body, (real courageous people, his apostles, holed up in a hiding place) but the people at the Carroll wake had to believe this one.

Like any small town, it seemed as if the story was out before the casket fell on Bill Carroll. Hundreds of people, who were supposed to be working, converged on the Carroll house. They were like the apostle Thomas. They wanted to see Bill Carroll and touch him in the flesh.

And the reporters from the area came with their cameramen. Pushing and shoving one another like papaparazzi, the cameramen barged in the house and tried to get the best angle on the newly raised while their reporters interviewed him. There were so many of them trying to interview him at the same time, however, that violence broke out among them when one cameraman hit another in the head with his camera.

In order to save his house from destruction and his wife, children, and grandchildren from being injured, Bill went out in the freezing cold and told the reporters he would talk to them and pose for pictures as long as they wanted, but only outside.

As Bill gave interviews with great generosity, hordes of people took out their scissors or hunting knives and began to cut out patches as holy relics from the suit he was laid out in. Within a few minutes, Bill was standing in his underwear, and some of them were beginning to cut his shorts and coming closer and closer to his private parts.

When the police arrived, they tried to calm the crowd and restore order, but the township had but a few officers, and the melee turned into a donnybrook which overwhelmed the custodians of law and order. In the midst of the assault, one of the brighter policemen grabbed Bill, put him in a cruiser, and drove off with him to the safety of the police station where he locked him in a cell.

I love to go to Irish wakes, and I had more fun at this one than any other wake I've been at. The doings at Bill Carroll's wake will be told in story and song and legend as long as the township lasts. They'll be better than any eulogy anyone could have given for Bill, and a hundred times better than any homily Father Minihan could have given even if he took liberty with the truth.

After the policeman took Bill, some of the reporters who had gotten their stories for the evening T.V. news program and others for their newspapers, went back to their offices to file them. After that, there was Jeremiah to find. They didn't know where he was at the moment, but they knew where he lived.

3.

Most people knew Jeremiah because he had done work at their houses. He was good at what he did, carpenter work, small plumbing and electrical jobs, painting, paperhanging, and even some minor sidewalk repairs. His charges were fair, and they knew he'd come back if they weren't satisfied with some part of the job. He was an honest man.

But people said he was a religious fanatic who believed he talked with the Lord, a "bible thumper" as they called him. Most of his customers made up errands to do when he came to their house, because if they stayed home, he'd quote the Bible at them all the time he was working. The Protestants didn't mind his preaching so much as the Catholics.

If there was anyone else in the area as good at what he did as Jeremiah, the Catholics would never have hired him. Even their priests, who golfed and took a drink and liked good food, didn't carry on like Jeremiah. All he talked about was religion. Never hell, fire, and damnation. He wasn't that kind, but still, religion. All the time religion, until he'd almost drive you mad.

"If you believe in the Lord Jesus Christ," Jeremiah had said to Mrs. O'Malley while he was taking her toilet out and replacing it with a new one, "you'll be saved. There's nothing as powerful as the mercy of God no matter how great a sinner you are."

'I don't consider myself a great sinner," Mrs. O'Malley said. "At my age, sure what could I do? I haven't had a bad thought in years, and even if I did, I haven't the opportunity to carry it out, though I'd love to try." She laughed at her own humor. It was that Irish humor she knew had come down from generations of immigrants, but it would be wasted on Jeremiah who was a pleasant, but serious man.

After he had disconnected all the pipes, Jeremiah pulled the toilet off the seal and set it down in the box that came with the new toilet. He was neat when he worked, and people were amazed they never had to clean up after he left. "Leaving a mess after you finish a beautiful job is like staining your soul after you've been freshly baptized," he used to say.

"Well, I guess I'm happy for you Mrs. O'Malley that you can feel that way. But Jesus said we have to pray and be watchful all the time. You're a great beauty, you know, and someone could be out there hoping to catch you off guard."

Mrs. O'Malley thought it would be wonderful if someone caught her off guard, or on guard for that matter. At the age of sixty-five and both her husband and his instrument lying useless in the cemetery for the last four years, she wouldn't mind a bit. She was glad he put the thought in her head.

Jeremiah himself wasn't a good looking man, but at her age, she'd settle for a strong man, and Jeremiah was that. Everyone in town knew the old story about his wife and Bill Carroll, so maybe he could be tempted, but she doubted it. She took a peek at herself in the mirror in the bathroom. Not bad, she agreed. A few wrinkles, but a handsome face and a substantial front that no man would be disappointed in.

Jeremiah took the seal for the new toilet and began to fit it to the base where the toilet would sit. He was even more particular about this part of the job, because if the seal wasn't set right, the toilet would leak, and he would be embarrassed by his poor workmanship.

"Too many people worry about sin," Jeremiah said. "Not that it's not important with the devil trying to tempt us all the time, and with him even tempting the Lord when he went up the mountain to pray, but what the Lord wants us to do is believe in him. Do you read the Bible much, Mrs. O'Malley?" Jeremiah never called his customers by their given name. He felt when you were working for someone, it was a mark of respect to use Mr. or Mrs.

"It's not my favorite book. There's too many "thee's" and "thou's" and "thy's" in there. Besides, Catholics don't read the Bible for the most part."

Jeremiah was satisfied with the seal, and he picked up the new toilet and set it on the seal. Then he began to connect the water pipe. "That's sad," Jeremiah said. "Some day you should read the gospel of John. You'll see over and over again that what the Lord's looking after is for us to believe in Him as our Saviour."

Mrs. O'Malley was bored with his religious talk. She thought it might lead somewhere if she listened to him instead of excusing herself to do errands, but even if it did, she'd go crazy listening to such blarney. Holy people were a pain in the ass.

"I have to go to the grocery store, Jeremiah. There are some things I need for supper. How much do I owe you? I'll leave a check on the kitchen counter."

Jeremiah got the pipe attached and was tightening it. "I don't have it figured out yet. I'll leave a bill on the counter, and you can mail it to me." Jeremiah was afraid a customer might not have enough money in her checking account to pay the bill that day, and she'd be embarrassed. So he always said they could send him a check.

"O.K." Mrs. O'Malley said. "Thank you, Jeremiah."

"Thank you for the business. The Lord bless you," he said as she left. "Thank you, Lord, for not leading me into temptation," he said to himself. Jeremiah wasn't an unobservant man.

God's interlude

Jeremiah might be on guard to preserve his virtue, but let me tell you, he was in little danger since he keeps himself well insulated from women other than Sarah. Mrs. O'Malley, who would have traded her virtue for a "go at it," had about as much hope of seducing Jeremiah as someone did of seducing Elizabeth of England.

4.

As soon as Jeremiah Bowman had set out with Naomi for Bill Carroll's corpse house, their boots squeaking on the hard packed snow and their breath shooting out alternating puffs of white smoke, Millicent Kingsford Burnside put on her coat and rubbers and brown hat and walked across the road to visit her sister, Sarah Kingsford Bowman.

She was tall and regal like Sarah, although not half so handsome, and as she often said to Sarah, if there were any such thing as divine guidance in this world, they would never have married beneath them, a Bowman and a Burnside, both of them men of no distinction. William Burnside was dead, and her two daughters, who lived in California, didn't visit her often.

"You should have taught them their Bible instead of sending them off to those fancy atheist schools," Jeremiah said to her one day when she was complaining about her daughters' lack of gratitude.

Millicent had walked out of their house, bristling at the "nerve you have, Jeremiah," and resolving "never to set foot in this house again.... if you're here," she remembered to add.

Millicent knocked on her sister's door and pushed it open in one movement, taking off her hat, coat, and rubbers and placing them in an orderly fashion in the vestibule closet. She was eighty years old, a year older than Sarah, but she felt it unbecoming to make any concessions either to age or to her body.

"Where's he gone with that child?" Millicent demanded as she walked into the kitchen and poured herself a cup of tea. "Doesn't he know it's five below zero and Naomi's toes will get frost bitten?" She clucked her tongue at Jeremiah's irresponsibility. "Someone ought to make him use a little sense instead of letting him do any crazy thing he wants to do." Millicent made inferences about her sister's lack of control over her husband whenever an opportunity arose.

"Bill Carroll died," Sarah said wistfully. "He and I started teaching together in 1922, the September after I finished my courses at Bucknell. He was a fine, fine man."

"You should have married him," Millicent said. "At least he did something with his life that a person could be proud of, unlike the two we married. My William was nothing but a peddler all his life, and your Jeremiah a handyman."

"Don't forget his farming," Sarah said, a note of praise in her voice. "We had plenty to eat when a great number of people were having a hard time of it in the thirties."

"Things have come to a poor pass when a person has to laud a man for putting food on the table." Even though Millicent remembered the depression well, she was reluctant to praise William Burnside for being a good provider. "We deserved a lot better than we got from life, I can tell you that," she said, refusing at the age of eighty to see her life in a more rosy complexion than she had experienced it. "We should have married well, Sarah. Papa warned us about marrying beneath our station, but we were too stubborn to listen to him, and look what became of us."

Sarah sipped her tea and listened with patience to her older sister, a thing she had learned to do since childhood. Millicent reminded her of the way their lives might have been if they had waited for men of promise to propose instead of fastening their fates to common men.

Words from a poem by John Greenleaf Whittier came to Sarah: "Of all sad words of tongue or pen/ the saddest are these, it might have been." She thought they would be an appropriate epitaph for Millicent's burial stone. Sarah herself had decided long ago that self pity was not only a waste of time, but an exercise in boredom.

Sarah saw her own life from another perspective. Through teaching, she had made her own contribution without benefit of her husband, while Millicent, on the other hand, had never worked.

Sarah's mind wandered while Millicent prattled on about life's injustice. She recalled her first class, fifty-five years ago, and how nervous she had been the day she stood behind a desk rather than sitting in front of it. It wasn't until late October of that year she felt somewhat confident.

As her sophomores came into the classroom, she felt both relief and joy. The freshmen who were leaving were pleasant students, causing her no discipline problems, but depressing her. The most charitable words she could think of to describe them were well intentioned, but slow.

No matter how much enthusiasm Sarah expended during class with her freshmen, she could not reach them. Teaching them poetry provided no reward for her nor insight for them as they returned her energy with blank faces. She felt weary, slogging through their minds like a field of mud.

The sophomore girls, on the other hand, were tenacious, listening and questioning for the entire forty-five minutes, fascinated by the way poets used words and felt the world around them. Except for an occasional comment to draw Sarah's attention, the boys thought poetry was a sissy subject, and so they spent the class lusting after Sarah's sculpted face, full figure, and violet eyes.

She was excited as the sophomores arrived. She was going to bring them into the world of a newly discovered poet, Emily Dickinson. It was 1922. Miss Dickinson had died only thirty-six years before, in 1886. Few people of her time had known she was a poet, and the most recent book of her poems, *The Single Hound,* had been published only eight years before. Most scholars believed there were hundreds more poems that her niece and literary heir, Martha

Dickinson Bianchi, had not yet published.

Sarah had decided she would begin with an easy poem, and if they could follow Dickinson's symbolism and metrics and metaphysical leaps of intellectual imagery, she would lead them on to Dickinson's more complex poetry.

"Please turn to page 175, to a poem by Emily Dickinson, who I think will be recognized in years to come as our greatest poet." She read the poem, for poetry was meant to be heard.

>These are the days when Birds come back-
>A very few - a Bird or two -
>To take a backward look.
>
>These are the days when skies resume
>The old - old sophistries of June -
>A blue and gold mistake.
>
>Oh fraud that cannot cheat the Bee -
>Almost thy plausibility
>Induces my belief.
>
>Till ranks of seeds their witness bear -
>And softly thro' the altered air
>Hurries a timid leaf.
>
>O Sacrament of summer days,
>Oh Last Communion in the Haze -
>Permit a child to join.

Thy sacred emblems to partake -
Thy consecrated bread to take
And thine immortal wine!

"As you can see," Sarah said, "there are six stanzas in the poem. Let's begin with the first stanza, and then try to understand how the second, third, and fourth stanzas are reinforcing what the poet is saying in the first stanza.

"Ask yourselves some questions. Why have the birds left? Where were they going? Why have a few, not all of them, come back? Are the words 'sophistries' and 'plausibility' in the second and third stanzas keys to the poem?"

"Maria?" Maria raised her hand for every question, and Sarah had to be careful not to allow her to inhibit some of the slower students. Maria's mind grasped subtleties without a struggle.

"The birds have gone south for the winter, but a few, hoping they would not have to leave, allow themselves to be seduced by an Indian summer such as we're enjoying now."

"Very intuitive," Sarah said.

Joyce raised her hand. She and Maria were very competitive. Both were trying to win the gold medal in English, and it would be a dificult choice for Sarah to make.

"I agree with Maria's observations," Joyce said. She was the more tactful of the two. "And the words 'sophistries' in the second stanza and 'plausibility' in the third stanza mean clever, but misleading. So what Miss Dickinson says is that Indian summer is deceptive because it tempts one to believe the cold weather will remain at bay for the fall and winter."

"Excellent," Sarah said.

"So the words 'fraud that cannot cheat the Bee' in the third stanza means that Indian summer cannot deceive another part of nature, like the bee?" Philip asked.

When any of her students didn't interpret the poem correctly, Sarah was gracious in the manner she answered them. She was afraid the wrong tone in her voice could discourage them from speaking out in class again.

"You've brought up a good point, Philip, so why don't we look at it? A few birds are deceived by Indian summer, and yet the bee is a part of nature like the birds, and he isn't deceived because the flowers are dying or dead, and the worker bee has nothing left to pollinate. But there's another sign of nature telling the birds to fly south like their companions."

Maria's hand was almost waving in Sarah's face. "Yes, Maria."

"It's in the fourth stanza. "And softly thro' the altered air/ Hurries a timid leaf.' 'Altered air' is the hint something ominous is on its way, and the falling 'timid leaf' is the reality that summer is over despite what seems to be."

Sarah didn't know whether Maria would be a teacher, but she would be an English scholar far beyond the mind of Sarah. "Well done, Maria."

"Now Janice," Sarah said, using her method of calling on a particular student to prevent a few from dominating the discussion, "what do you think of the last two stanzas. Dickinson is changing her imagery here, is she not?"

"Well," Janice said, fearful of making a mistake, "we have communion in our church where we eat the bread, but they don't let us drink the wine. I know some churches do, but our church doesn't. Maybe she's trying to make nature holy or something like that."

"Ah," Sarah said, "I think you have given us a wonderful insight into the poem." Then Sarah guided her students through Dickinson's use of the images of nature, and how the poet transcended them by juxtaposing them with religious imagery to raise her experience of nature to a mystical experience far beyond earthly eyes.

Classes like this made life worthwhile for Sarah. It

was her religion, the embrace of beautiful minds in moments of rapture.

Like so many women in those days, Millicent had decided her status in society would be decided by her husband's position, and in Millicent's estimation, it was nothing much. Sarah tried to console her sister by reminding her that she had educated her girls well and that life was much better for them because of her, but this did not alleviate Millicent's sense of injustice that she was just a thread on the bottom of a quilt. Besides, her daughters had never included her in their lives, even less so since they had married. In retribution, Millicent never concerned herself about their accomplishments.

"Did you tell him not to go making a fool of himself in front of that Carroll family? He's likely to go in there and start preaching to them about the Lord's will and heaven and the final judgment and all that other nonsense. Oh, my God, he'll make us the laughing stock of the whole countryside," Millicent said in frustration.

"Mary Carroll likes Jeremiah, I think. At least he's done a number of repairs in her house," Sarah said.

"She's a Catholic, isn't she?" Millicent said. "And if they hear a word of public prayer coming out of anyone's mouth but a priest's, they think it's some kind of devil worship. Jeremiah will start praying as soon as he's there five minutes."

Sarah looked out the window, the snow falling, lightly, but falling as it seemed to do every day in January until some days it got so cold that it seemed too cold even for snow.

She thought her memory was failing a bit, and yet she could picture Bill Carroll when he was young, a handsome, hard-bodied man, "blonde in hair and blue in eye," as the first poem she wrote about him read awkwardly, and she remembered how it felt to be young and in love. He was taller than she was, and that in itself was remarkable luck, for both Millicent and she were too tall for almost every boy and man they had ever liked.

And Bill Carroll had liked her. They comforted one another about their anxious first year of teaching. Together they read the love poetry of Donne and Shakespeare and Marvell, and they seduced one another while reading aloud Marvell's "To His Coy Mistress." It seemed to Sarah as though she and Bill were to live happily ever after, that is until his family found out about their interest in each other.

The Carrolls were Catholic, tracing their ancestry to the famous Carrolls of Maryland, and a Catholic didn't marry a Protestant in 1924 unless he was very strong and determined, and Bill Carroll, as it turned out, was neither. Her own father was against her marrying a Catholic, but she knew she could have persuaded him if Bill had had the courage to stand up to his clan.

They had begun their romance without benefit of marriage. It started their very first year of teaching when they were chosen to go to Harrisburg for a conference on teaching poetry to high school students. The conference was for three days, and the first night Bill had made his way to her hotel room on the pretense of discussing some of the day's agenda, and she had let him in on the pretense of being interested in discussing the day's agenda.

He had brought wine, a Beringer Chardonnay, hoping she would join him in drinking the bottle. And she had ordered some cheese and crackers from room service, hoping he might come to her room and that she would have something to offer him so he would stay awhile.

After they had drunk some wine and eaten some cheese and crackers, they sat on the couch next to one another, and he read from a book of poems which he carried with him.

> Had we but world enough, and time,
> This coyness, lady, were no crime.....

She smiled, because unlike the lady in the poem, she was more than willing to forego the state of maidenhood.

> An hundred years should go to
> praise
> Thine eyes, and on thy forehead
> gaze;
> Two hundred to adore each breast,
> But thirty thousand to the rest.

As he read the poetry in his warm, resonant voice, she began to feel herself grow flushed, and she moved closer to him and put her head on his shoulder. Her body was moist and churning. She was a romantic, passionate about poetry and novels that told of love lost or to be discovered. She knew the poem he was reading by heart, Marvell's "To His Coy Mistress," and she smiled again as she thought of the lines to come: grasp the moment, for when you are dead, you are dead to all such feeling and all such promise of love.

> But at my back I always hear
> Time's winged chariot hurrying near;
> And yonder all before us lie
> Deserts of vast eternity.
> Thy beauty shall no more be found,
> Nor, in thy marble vault, shall sound
> My echoing song; then worms shall
> try
> That long-preserved virginity,
> And your quaint honor turn to dust,
> And into ashes all my lust.
> The grave's a fine and private place,
> But none, I think, do there embrace.

Bill Carroll was not taking advantage of Sarah. She was a willing partner. She would grasp this moment and savor it for the time of her life. There would be no other moment again, she was sure, like this moment.

> Now therefore, while thy youth
> Sits on thy skin like morning dew,
> And while thy willing soul transpires
> At every pore with instant fires,
> Now let us sport us while we may,
> And now, like amorous birds of prey,
> Rather at once our time devour
> Than languish in his slow-chapped power.
> Let us roll all our strength and all
> Our sweetness up into one ball,
> And tear our pleasures with rough strife
> Through the iron gates of life.
> Thus, though we cannot make our sun
> Stand still, yet we will make him run.

What she remembered most and loved most about Bill Carroll was the reverence he brought to the act of love, his tenderness, his praising her body, even pausing to lift his glass of wine in toasting her hair and eyes and breasts and legs and thighs. Like a master of some long-forgotten religious ritual, he made a ceremony of the holy act of love. He moved about her body on his hands and knees as if he were kneeling before a shrine, gently kissing, touching gently, gently moving into her sacred depths, a hallowed moment of mystery.

Never in her life had she or would she experience such a holy rite of passage, such passion that was like religious ecstasy, like Leda caught up by the god Zeus. Lines from Yeat's poem kept walking through her mind. "Being so caught up/ so mastered by the brute blood of the air/ Did she put on his knowledge with his power....?"

Bill Carroll knew her now even as Sarah knew him. They were bound by this mystic night, and her memory of the mood may have been even more immense than her memory of the deed.

Whenever they could meet, they did, but the times were few since both of them lived at home. They managed to go to conferences together, but they were infrequent. And no matter how much Bill protested his love, he didn't have the courage to choose Sarah over his family.

Perhaps, as with most things, their passion had been magnified in her eyes by the passage of time, but she didn't think so. Those moments were for her like one of James Joyce's epiphanies, a manifestation of grace and beauty that transcends this world of time and space.

Sarah was a passionate woman, but Jeremiah was a perfunctory lover. For some reason, he hurried, leaving her behind, until one day she told him he wasn't going about their lovemaking the right way. Jeremiah might have thought she was drawing on her experience with Bill Carroll, which everyone knew about, but he listened to her and did well enough to satisfy her. She refused to go through life with sex that held no pleasure.

"Maybe it's a good thing you never married Bill," Millicent said, never forgetting the past in favor of the present. "You could have ended up with eight children like Mary Carroll and be just as plump."

Sarah turned and looked at Millicent, her face angry

for a moment, and then subsiding into a faint smile. "You may be right."

If she had married him, she would never have taught, for pregnant teachers had to take long leaves of absence that would have gone on for years with so many children. And would they have read poetry to each other after the fourth or the fifth or sixth child had wearied her? And would their moments of love have become stale and dreary and rote? Would their couplings have become hurried in fear of a child waking and jiggling the doorknob to their bedroom?

No fine wine. No hallowed ground. No mystery. No holy ritual. No ecstasy. As things had turned out, sordid reality could not take away the memory of their ceremony of innocence. Perhaps her first love was like the work of an artist, forever enshrined, beyond the graffiti of time.

"Anna," Millicent said, "you shouldn't eat so much. You're getting as round as a silo, and no man's going to want a huge woman for a wife." Millicent held her cup of tea with great delicacy, but by a singular act of dexterity, she managed to extend her index finger in Anna's direction. "A man will put up with a wife that gets fat after he marries her, especially if she complains she's stretched out from bearing his children, but before marriage he wants a slim lady."

Anna took her fourth soft boiled egg and cracked it open on a piece of crisp toast, mashing the yolk until it had saturated the toast and then shaking cascades of salt and pepper over it. She liked her aunt Millicent and enjoyed listening to her strange concern about people and things, even about Anna herself.

She had had the child for her parents, and that was all she was going to do. Why her aunt couldn't accept that was puzzling to her. "Everyone should make her life a statement," her father had said, and she had made her statement when she gave birth to Naomi. From that moment there would be no more statements.

She didn't want to be like her mother or her father or

her aunt Millicent or anyone else. Since she was not intense about life, she decided the best thing to do about it was nothing, and to occupy her time while she was doing nothing, she ate.

"He wants them to erect a statue in memory of his good deeds," Sarah said, interrupting Millicent who never seemed to mind being interrupted. "He says he'll go to the township meeting and propose it to the township supervisors."

Millicent sipped at her tea and smiled because she knew that Sarah could not have said Jeremiah Bowman wanted a statue erected in his honor.

"Don't you let Jeremiah Bowman bring a statue in this house," Millicent said. "He'll have the whole township saying you turned Catholic, bowing down to a heap of plaster."

"You heard me," Sarah said, irritated at her sister's habit of misunderstanding whatever she found unpleasant. Millicent would like to cancel their husbands and even their children if that would help erase "their marrying down" as she put it. All the embarrassing things that had happened to them in their lifetime could be traced to God's punishment for that dreadful deed. "He's lived a holy life, he says, and he wants a statue, not for himself, but to honor such a way of life. He said God spoke to him and told him what to do."

Sarah could see where it would lead, the snickering and the name calling and the shame. She would like to throw her body across his path to stop his mad pursuit, but she was unable to do that.

Despite their differences and arguments about their opposing views on life, she loved him, not with the youthful passion she had once had for Bill Carroll, but with an abiding love nonetheless.

"Now, Sarah, you must be mistaken. Even that husband of yours would never do such a thing." But Millicent knew he was capable of anything, and she wondered if she shouldn't be content with erasing the future rather than the past. "He'll make us the butt of every joke in the township. Sarah, we're Kingsfords, the original settlers in this township."

Millicent liked to remind Sarah of what she already knew. "He's going to make every Kingsford interred in Gate of Heaven cemetery for the last two hundred years a mockery." Millicent shook her head in sorrow. "The trouble with being a Kingsford woman is you not only lose the name, but you bring impurities into the line."

"I've been trying to talk him out of it," Sarah said, "but he's as single-minded as a bee in a flower. I know he hears me, but he doesn't listen to me."

"I don't know why you never divorced the man," Millicent sighed. "He's brought the family nothing but shame." She knew of Sarah's liaison, of course, but other Kingsford women had had affairs over the years, and she saw little problem with that as long as they were discrete. Millicent took it as a sign of their sense of adventure, not of their lack of morals. She would have had an affair of her own, if asked, but she hadn't been.

"A Kingsford never divorces," Sarah said. "You know that better than I do. Never in this township in two hundred years has a Kingsford divorced."

"You're right," Millicent conceded. "That would be the same as saying a Kingsford made a mistake." She looked at Anna, who was now eating her sixth egg mashed into a piece of toast. She was happy her niece was a Bowman.

Allah's Interlude

Where in heaven can I hide when Millicent gets here? She's wonderful to Sarah, and I praise her for that. But most of the time she prattles on like a katy-did, and I can't stand their shrill sound any more than I can hers. And neither of them ever varies its song, the same high pitched tone all night long. Sometimes it keeps me awake.

I guess that's the reason I don't like the hot weather. When the cold comes, the male katy-dids stop moving their forewings which make that awful noise. I don't know what I was thinking of when I made them.

Although, honest to me, not even the cold nor daylight stops Millicent. I think I'll team her up with John the Baptist and Jerome. She'd fit right in with those two, prattling all day long.

John the Baptist spends his whole day trying to get people to repent and let him pour water over their heads, and Jerome tells everyone he's the one who translated the Bible. Sometimes I think if I let John open a fastfood outlet which sold only locusts and let Jerome collect royalties on his translations, they'd be happy as "birthday boys."

Millicent's poor William is up here, free at last from that chattering magpie. He sits in the light all day long, silent and content, reading mystery stories, dreading the day she dies. Each time I run into him, he says, "Lord, bestow on her the gift of being the oldest woman who ever lived." On other days, he'll say, "Lord, give me the power to grow a beard so she won't recognize me when she gets here."

I remember Sarah when she was a young woman, and let me tell you, of all women born of women, she had to be one of the most lovely I have ever seen, and I've seen them all. I always thought that Bill Carroll was a mutton head when he didn't marry Sarah.

Why Sarah was like Helen of Troy. Menelaus, the

Greek King, started a war that lasted ten years to get his wife Helen back from the Trojan, Paris, and that mousey Bill wouldn't even buck his Irish family to marry Sarah. Remember the mighty line of Christopher Marlowe about Helen: "Is this the face that launched a thousand ships?" Bill was no Menelaus, but Sarah was as beautiful as Helen. He deserved what he got, a frump, not a bad person, mind you, but a frump.

I'm all knowing, but sometimes I think I'm not so smart. Here I am, a pure spirit, perfect in myself, but I don't know anything about the pleasures of sex I've given to men and women. Even in mythology, old Zeus, the lecher, was seducing every woman in sight, and I'm still wondering what I'm missing.

I don't know how my son resisted all those black eyed, olive skinned, hot-blooded women he got to know on earth when he had an earthly body, but he was single-minded about his mission of redemption. If it had been me, I sure would have been tempted. I'd stay on my diet, of course, but I'd look over the menu.

I'm going to tell you a secret. It won't ruin the novel for you, I promise. Jeremiah and Bill are both going to die before Sarah. Just because Bill was raised from the dead doesn't mean he's not going to die. My son raised Lazarus, and he died. It's the way things go when you're human. Even my Son died.

It will be interesting to get everyone who knows the three of them to wager a bet on which one Sarah chooses to show her around heaven when she gets here. I'll put my money on Jeremiah. I know you think the odds will be on Bill, her first true love, but I'll put my money on Jeremiah.

Sarah committed fornication, and it's a sin against my sixth commandment, but I still like her. David committed a worse sin, adultery, with Bathsheba, and he sent her husband, Uriah, to the front lines of battle to be killed, so he could have Bathsheba all to himself. And David is still my beloved.

They brought the woman caught in adultery before my Son, and he told them to stone her for what she did if they had no sin on their own conscience. They had to walk away without so much as throwing a pebble.

But as bad as all their sins were, they repented, and no sin is greater than my mercy. If you want to read David's wondrous song of repentance, it's Psalm fifty-one. This is the way it begins: "Have mercy on me, Oh God, according to your steadfast love; according to your abundant mercy, blot out my transgressions." What a mensch, that David!

My editor tells me I have to stick another chapter in here to tell you about Sarah and Jeremiah's marriage, so I'll do it, but I can't wait to tell you what happens when the reporters and cameramen and crowds arrive at Sarah and Jeremiah's home. My editor used to write for the New Yorker magazine, so he thinks he's the bee's knees. He is good though, or I wouldn't have hired him. His initials are E.B.W.

5.

When Sarah Kingsford accepted Jeremiah Bowman's proposal of marriage, there were people who refused to believe she would do such a thing. Even after they saw her picture in the society section of the Sunday newspaper and they believed it because they had seen the announcement and read the piece, they couldn't understand it.

The Kingsford family had been in America for two hundred years when Sarah had been born, and the name of every family member and his or her line of descendants was researched by Jonathan Kingsford, Sarah's father, and etched by a woodcarver into its proper chronological niche in a large paneled wall in his library.

Jonathan Kingsford had not found himself in a generous financial situation as had many other Kingsfords because his father, Matthias Kingsford, had been a poor businessman. As long as he had the blood and the large family home which his father had inherited from Jonathan's successful grandfather, however, he was well satisfied since he had wanted to be a professor at a University, and if his father's business had prospered, he would have felt obliged to carry on what his father had begun.

By his wife, Constance, herself a woman of vaunted lineage, Jonathan had two daughters, Millicent, and then a year later, Sarah. It grieved him that he had no male heirs to carry his surname, but his several cousins had seven boys among their children, and that was enough to assure the Kingsford name would endure a long time. If he had lived during a time when it was acceptable, he would have encouraged his girls not to surrender the Kingsford name when they married.

"But who is he?" Jonathan asked Sarah when she had told him about Jeremiah. "What is his social....?"

"His pedigree?" Sarah interrupted. "Not much better

than a mongrel pup, I'm afraid." She had never been able to enshrine the family line with awe, which would have pleased her father, and she thought some of her best writings, when she was trying to get published, were satires against the Brahmin caste of American society. 'In a democracy,' she had written, "the only pedigrees should be those attested to by the American Kennel Club."

"I do hope you'll be kind to him, Father," Sarah said, holding his left arm with both her hands and kissing his cheek. "He's a good man. Not a cultivated man, perhaps, but a good man. I think he'll make me happy."

"I'm happy for you if he's a good man, Sarah," Jonathan said, himself a man not given to causing pain. "But the township expects a Kingsford to marry someone of, shall I say, gentle birth. You see, Sarah," he said patting her hands to comfort her as he spoke, "people of common lineage need an ideal as it were, something beyond them, like a star, perhaps, to which they can look up and aspire to and on which they can dream."

"Like wishing on a star, you mean, Father?" Sarah asked, hoping that her gentle irony might dissuade him from a pompous catalogue of America's need for its Brahmins.

"Not exactly, dear Sarah," he said, pausing for a moment in hope of finding a compelling image that might persuade her. "People are jealous of their equals, of one or another of their friends' having more than they. But people consider the very rich and the very cultivated beyond envy because they feel their worlds are totally disparate from that of ordinary humans."

Jonathan felt more confident in his argument as he progressed. "Life is too real for them, and so they look to us to present the Platonic Ideal, that to which they can aspire, but never reach, like pilgrims offering homage at a shrine."

Jonathan kissed Sarah on her cheek as if he were consoling her before his final thrust which would assure his victory. "And so it is our responsibility, dear Sarah, to remain in our lighthouse in order that people below us might see the beacon that shines above them."

Sarah was certain that Beacon Hill and the beacon in North Church and Paul Revere were all entangled like a mixed metaphor in her father's thoughts. He was a good man and a good father, but one born out of due time, an anachronism.

"Your sister, Millicent," Jonathan continued, "married William Burnside, who was also, according to Millicent, a good man, but it hardly seems to have made her happy now, does it?" Jonathan walked to the mantle where he kept his pipes and selected a very long black briar that he was convinced helped him to think more clearly.

"You're a graduate of Bucknell, my dear girl, a certified teacher, and a lover of poetry and music and art. To whom will you read your beloved Emily Dickinson? The very swiftness of her thought would preclude such poems being understood by this Jeremiah of yours."

"There was another man I loved, Father," Sarah began heatedly, but regained her composure. The loss of one's equanimity, her father used to say, is tantamount to the loss of one's civility. "I lost Bill because of your prejudice against Catholics, and now you'd like me to give up Jeremiah because of his lack of pedigree. Wouldn't it be easier for both of us if you did the choosing for me?"

Sarah was fudging the truth because she would have married Bill despite all her father's objections. Bill was the one who had refused to marry her. Sarah had come to her Father in perfect peace, but within a few minutes, he had scattered her composure.

"Now, Sarah," he said, puffing with intense pleasure on his pipe, "Mr. Carroll is a Catholic, and we Kingsfords simply don't marry Catholics. Look at your heritage," he said, pointing his pipe at the Kingsford genealogy chiseled into the wall. "In all these two hundred years, never has a Kingsford married a Catholic. It would have been unthinkable for you, my own daughter, to be the first.

"And Catholics, especially Irish Catholics, spend an unconscionable amount of time sinning and then grieving over their sins. The only Catholic group worse than the Irish," he said, "are the Italians, and a liaison with one of them would cause every Kingsford to rise from the grave in outrage."

"I'm going to marry Jeremiah," Sarah said in defiance. "He's a good man, and he's a Protestant."

"My God, Sarah, a Protestant, a real Protestant, is either Anglican in England or Episcopalian in America. Our church is structured by Bishops, by learned men who have studied long years." Jonathan Kingsford shook his head in perplexity, but he kept his voice level and reasonable.

"A Baptist sings and preaches with passion enough to disturb the harmony of the most placid God. He must hate to listen to one of their congregation's having services."

Sarah knew her father wasn't prejudiced against Baptists in particular, merely against passion versus reason. He was a neo-classical man who had been born one century too late, and according to him, all religious groups in America were victims not of society's prejudice, but of their own lack of control.

"I'm going to marry him, Father. I'll take a ring from him on Christmas Eve." Sarah stood straight, her tall figure held aloft with elegance as Jonathan had encouraged her to do.

He grieved in silence at her words. Sarah had too fine a mind, too exquisite a nature to waste it on any man in this bereft Lackawanna Valley, but he had no means with which to introduce her to New York or Philadelphia or Boston society, even though he had social connections in all of those cities. It had been all he could manage to send her to Bucknell for her teacher's degree, and he remembered in pain that she had not bought a single new dress in the years she had been away.

She must have suffered remarks from other girls he couldn't bear to think about. If she was determined to marry this cliff dweller, this troglodyte, he would not take the chance of alienating her. Of his two daughters, Sarah was his favorite. Millicent was tall and carried herself well, but she was average looking and sluggish of mind. The quickness of Sarah's mind excited him, and her ability to match his arguments and even to better him was his greatest pleasure, a secret which, however, he kept from her.

"I've told you what I think," he said, submitting to her, knowing he had argued with reason and had ventured as much in demanding she obey him as he dared.

Sarah smiled politely, but not triumphantly. 'The worst of all civilized sins is vanity in victory,' her father had often said. She could hear the solemn tone of his voice as he spoke these words.

Jonathan was an elegant man, very tall and very erect, a carriage he was proud his daughters had emulated. Sarah had often cried because she was so tall, but he proclaimed that height was a sign of grandeur, and he insisted she take ballet lessons to learn to walk with regal grace and distinguished carriage, accentuating her height until she learned to carry herself with pride.

Constance Kingsford died when Millicent and Sarah were still not of school age, and despite the protests of several of Constance's sisters who thought the girls needed female guidance and offered to raise them, Jonathan resolved to assume the complete responsibility of caring for his daughters.

Although he was an Episcopalian and although he took his daughters to services every Sunday, Jonathan regarded religion as a refinement of civilization, somewhat on the level of poetry, an elegance in living that a cultivated person should observe. He expected his pastor to preach sermons that did not offend reason.

"Preaching a sermon on hell insults not only my intelligence, but your own, Reverend Downey," Jonathan telligence, but your own, Reverend Downey," Jonathan had said in greeting the rector after a Sunday service. "To attribute more mercy to men who punish for only a time than to God Who you say punishes forever unmasks the primitive in your character. Good day to you, sir."

Millicent and Sarah didn't know whether they should hide their faces in shame at their father's blunt observations or giggle at the Reverend Downey's open-mouthed astonishment.

As they were returning to their home, Jonathan said, "You must never hold a grudge, my daughters. If something need not be said, then for the sake of kindness and harmony, don't say it. If something must be said, on the other hand, speak your mind with honesty and civility, but never with anger. A cultivated person never surrenders to his emotions. Such loss of control is barbarian."

After dinner which Jonathan prepared with a minimum of culinary skill, he took his cigar, a small glass of liqueur, (generally Amaretto because he enjoyed the almond flavor and the warm sensation it caused in his stomach) Millicent, and Sarah into his study where he expounded on his philosophy, which, of course, he wished to become their philosophy.

"I don't have the money my cousins have," he said on one occasion, "and I regret that for your sake. But I have other things which I can leave you as my inheritance, like education and knowledge and intelligence and wisdom and refinement and taste. I will expose your minds to the classics and poetry and linguistics and science and art and music. You will excel in culture and learning, and from that lofty height, you may observe the monetary wealth of your cousins with serene detachment."

With each session he enhanced their sense of being unique, even chosen, and they acquired his pride in their lineage and their learning. "He was a man born out of due time," Sarah often observed, "but he was a wonderful father for very young, motherless girls, and I loved him as much as any daughter could love her father."

"Having to sell the house killed him," Millicent said. "When the new owners saw the paneling and talked about how they could sand out the entire family genealogy and refinish the wood until it was like new, that was the end. He cried that night," Millicent said in a husky voice, trying not to cry herself. "It was the first time in my life I saw him cry."

"It was more than that," Sarah knew. "You and I, Millicent. You and I. We didn't marry in the Kingsford tradition, and that hurt him every bit as much."

The township people agreed that Sarah was "marrying down," that Jeremiah, a mere handyman, was no catch for anyone, let alone a Kingsford.

But as some of the women said at the weekly gathering of the quilt-makers, "the pickins in the area aren't plentiful for someone like a Kingsford, and a poor one at that. There's not much of a dowry there."

"And besides, everybody knows she's been around the block."

"She and Bill Carroll never fooled anyone. There were a lot of other teachers at those Harrisburg conferences, and they talked."

"She's not getting any younger, either. She'll be twenty-seven pretty soon."

"Even so, you might have thought she could have done a lot better than Jeremiah Bowman."

"I think they met at play practice with the New Theater Group."

"Sarah had a part in the play, and Jeremiah was on the stage crew."

"You have to admit she's a beautiful woman."

"With a nice figure. Any man would be tempted."

"And some gave in."

"And so did she."

They all laughed.

The day Sarah married Jeremiah, a day filled with spring and lilacs, Jonathan Kingsford was distraught. No matter how well he conducted himself, the scandal of his daughters' marriages would cause him embarrassment all his life. The family of Kingfords treated children who strayed and their parents with a condescension and tolerance that was as severe a punishment as excommunication for a Catholic.

Sarah wanted a large wedding, and though the expense was one reason Jonathan tried to dissuade her, the more important was that he didn't want large numbers of Kingsfords descending on him, their faces expressing both sympathy and ridicule. They would come to the wedding. They were loyal to that extent, but their fiercest loyalty was to the family, not to a particular member of it.

Millicent had eloped. Jonathan had taken an intractable stand against her marrying William Burnside who was far beneath her position, a peddler at best, but Millicent married despite his disapproval. He couldn't understand her reasoning.

Even though William was a decent sort of man, Millicent never seemed to like him. Perhaps, because she was twenty-six, not very attractive, and not very popular, she took the first offer that came. Throughout the centuries, all Kingsford women had married, and she may have been afraid to be the first who didn't, a place in the family history she had no intention of occupying.

He admired Millicent for her carriage and her manners, but she was a fuss about the house, cleaning and scrubbing, especially the bathrooms, and he had on many occasions sat on a damp toilet seat because of her domestic zeal. She reminded him of a bird, pecking about, searching for something to set in order, obsessed about the horizontal posture of pictures on the walls, a speck of dust on a table, or a minute stain on the tablecloth. Her scurrying annoyed him.

Like most educated men, especially professors, Jonathan Kingsford loved conversation spiced with irony, satire, and wit, but when he engaged in such linguistic gymnastics with Millicent, he met with abject failure. Not only did she not understand the subtleties of language, but she found them unsuited to her domestic concerns.

"Father," she complained, "you and Sarah can amuse yourselves with your word games, but the perfect truth is that nothing would get done in this house if it were left to the two of you. If you spent as much time devising ways to earn money as you do devising ways to amuse your mind, life would be much more comfortable around here."

Millicent had two things on her mind, money and cleanliness, Jonathan thought, neither of which he found worthy of commanding lifelong devotion. And so when she had married William Burnside because he had 'excellent prospects' as Millicent put it and had eloped because she was afraid Jonathan would stop the marriage, he was relieved. "No more damp toilet seats" was the first thing he said to himself upon entering his bathroom, although on further reflection, he was ashamed of his cynical musing.

The Kingsfords understood her eloping as they understood the parable of the prodigal. It was to be expected, they believed, that not everyone in the line would be loyal, and that they must allow for defectors. Millicent, because of her initial defiance and despite her eventual repentance and contrition, was classified by the Kingsfords as a defector.

She grew so penitent that she would have gone before them in sackcloth and ashes, but once fallen, the Kingsfords forgave in their civilized ways, but they did not forget the blight on the family name. To forget, as they reminded one another, was to risk taking lightly another family member's fall from grace. Be lenient once, and the family structure would crumble.

Jonathan Kingsford had contemplated suicide on several occasions before April 24th, the day of Sarah's wedding, and his future son-in-law, Jeremiah, was responsible for his feeling of despondency.

"An Episcopalian minister?" Jeremiah asked with curiosity. "The Reverend Harry Downey? Well, that's all right with me," he said, "just so long as he knows he won't be conducting the marriage service or reading from his prayer book. We'll put him down as an expert witness, and he can even file the marriage certificate to make it legal if he wants."

"My good man," Jonathan said, trying to be as patient as he would with an unruly student, "you simply don't understand. The Kingsfords are Episcopalians, and they are to be married by an Episcopalian minister. Pastor Downey is not simply a witness. He performs the marriage ceremony. It's always been that way in our family."

"Whatever marrying's done on the 24th of April," Jeremiah said, his face breaking into a smile as Sarah walked into the room, "Sarah and I, we'll be the ones doing it. Sarah's going to say she'll take me for her lawful wedded husband, that she'll love, honor, and respect me until death do us part, and I'm going to say the same thing to her. And that'll marry us. Then I'm going to give a little talk on what it means to marry."

Jonathan looked at the wall of Kingsfords, the names from generation after generation, and wondered how one uneducated, gawky, skinny young man had the boldness to defy their tradition. A third generation American at best, of peasant stock, an uneducated handyman, and a religious fanatic capable of a public display of emotion were more than he deserved at the hands of his distant God.

"My dear young man," Jonathan said, "our family feels and has always felt there is a certain decorum that a minister lends to such an occasion, and if you could see our point of view, it would make things so much more pleasant." He could see Sarah's suppressing a smile, and he knew she would not help him.

"I'm afraid I can't do that, Mr. Kingsford," Jeremiah said, bowing and shaking his head as if he were sad the request was impossible to grant. "Anything else you want, sir, I'm agreeable to, but marrying is too holy to let other people do it for you. Now I'll have to say good day to you sir. I have a kitchen I'm remodeling for Mrs. Hawkins, and she's going to be awful upset if I don't show up. Goodbye Sarah." And with that, he left.

Jonathan, Sarah, and Millicent went to the large sun room and began opening the replies to the wedding invitations and counting the number of those who would attend. Jonathan grew more and more distraught as it became apparent that none of the Kingsfords had any previous engagements for that day and all of them were coming to the wedding.

"You shouldn't marry that man," Millicent said in the commanding tone of an older sister. "I married William Burnside, and I've never stopped regretting it. He's a good man and a good provider, but he's not one of us. And if it's hard to be married to a man of no breeding, then it's going to be twice as bad to be married to an uncultured man who is a religious fanatic."

"I think I'll grow to love him, Millicent," Sarah said, used to her sister's direct way of speaking. "The Kingsford tradition is pretentious. I'm sorry, father, but it is, and rather ludicrous at times. He's a simple, unaffected man, and he's honest and reliable. And he's a Protestant, father, unlike Bill Carroll," she added pointedly.

"Sarah, there are many differences between you and this man," Jonathan said, now that Millicent had begun the argument, "especially the religious one. Religion with us has been a matter of form, fitting and proper for a Sunday morning. It's a nice thing, religion, but nothing to become passionate about. With this man of yours it appears to be a passion.

"You have nothing in your background to understand such a fixation, let alone enter into it. And furthermore, you have a brilliant mind, and he's unable to be an intellectual companion for you. I've told you that before."

"I want a change, father," Sarah said, "and I haven't noticed too many eligible suitors knocking at your door to ask for my hand. I'm twenty-seven years old, and I'd like to have a family.

"I'll always have my teaching to keep my mind alert, and you, of course, but I need something real in my life, or I'm going to live it artificially, like those names on the library wall. I don't want to end up there, father, and I'm not saying that to hurt you."

"You're a young fool," Millicent said, bitterness creeping into her voice. "I look at William sitting across the table from me, just the two of us, and I wonder how I could have sold the Kingsford heritage for money and a good, but ordinary man."

"It's an affair of the heart," Sarah said, laughing aside their fears. "I love him for his tenderness and his goodness, and I can handle his strange religious ways."

And so the wedding took place, and the noble Kingsfords sat on the bride's side of the Church and the ordinary Bowmans sat on the groom's side, and the Reverend Harry Downey was only an expert witness to the ceremony. When Jeremiah Bowman and Sarah Kingsford turned to the congregation and said in unison, "we now declare us man and wife," there was a loud hush that fell over the Kingsfords, but nothing like the stunned air of disbelief when Jeremiah Bowman walked up into the pulpit. The Reverend Harry Downey bowed his head and stared into the *Book of Common Prayer*, and Jonathan Kingsford slumped noticeably in the front pew.

"There's a lot of folks here who were never at a wedding where the groom did the talking, I guess, but that'll be all changed after today," Jeremiah said, forcing himself to stand up straighter than he liked to stand. He was much more comfortable in a slouch, but he wanted everyone to be able to see him. "I wanted to tell you something that only Sarah and me would know and not the minister or her father or her sister or any of my family either.

"What you just heard and what you just saw was something you should pray to God will happen to each one of your children. You heard Sarah and me say we'd marry each other and we'd stay married forever as long as there was life in either one of us.

"And it doesn't make any difference whether the times are good or bad or whether the Lord gives us a lot of children or no children. It just matters that we said it because it's a holy thing to get married, and we said it in front of all of you so that there'll always be someone who remembers we said it, and we said it in front of God if no one else remembers.

"And you witnessed today the same kind of holy thing as all my folks witnessed when I was plunged in the waters of the Baptist Church and made a servant of God."

The Reverend Harry Downey and the Kingsfords cringed at the unseemly and ungainly image of this lanky man being immersed in a large tub of water, and those among them who had been involved in extra-marital affairs were uncomfortable at the idea that this wretched creature might be preaching to them.

"And I won't keep you here any longer except to say this final word to you." Jeremiah bowed his head as if he were beseeching the Lord to help him in the task he had set for himself. "From this day on and forward, with a woman at my side so beautiful that it's hard to imagine she would even give me a glance, like I've been trying to do in the past, I'm going to live with only the Lord figuring as the example I've got to follow. I'm setting out to be a saint."

The Kingsfords were composed in the most difficult of situations. They prided themselves on keeping their emotions under control like the English gentry from whom they were descended, but an involuntary gasp and then a repentant silence came from the bride's side of the church at the mention of the word "saint."

The Reverend Harry Downey looked up from the

Book of Common Prayer, and he had a startled, hurt look on his face as though he had been invited to a party and the host had deliberately spilled a drink on him. The air smacked of Rome and statues and idolatry, and the Kingsfords felt ravished as if each one of them had suffered the bridal bed.

Sarah was the only Kingsford who was at peace and who enjoyed the discomfort of her high born kinsmen. If the Kingsfords had any sense among them, she thought, they would realize Jeremiah had been carried away by the joy of the moment.

In all seriousness, no one could think Jeremiah meant he was going to spend his life in the pursuit of sainthood like some Catholic. Life didn't work that way. Passion was for the marriage bed, not for religion. Her marriage to him would turn out just fine.

But her marriage had turned out to be more strange that she could have imagined. She loved his loving her so much, but he annoyed her with his preaching and praying. He was such an unrestrained servant of the Lord that at time she thought he should be put in restraints.

Trying to integrate his love of God with her love of poetry, she read him the holy sonnets of John Donne, since few poets had written poems of such religious depth. Her favorite was Donne's great paradoxical sonnet:

> Batter my heart, three personed God;
> for You
> as yet but knock, breathe, shine, and
> seek to mend;
> That I may rise and stand, o'erthrow
> me, and bend
> Your force, to break, blow, burn, and
> make me new.

> I, like an usurped town, to another due,
> Labor to admit You, but Oh, to no end!
> Reason, Your viceroy in me, me should defend,
> But is captive, and proves weak or untrue.
> Yet dearly I love You, and would be loved fain,
> But am bethrothed unto Your enemy:
> Divorce me, untie or break that knot again,
> Take me to You, imprison me, for I,
> Except You enthrall me, never shall be free,
> Nor ever chaste, except You ravish me.

Sarah thought Jeremiah would be captivated as she was by the amazing paradox of the last line, but he found the image of the poet's pleading for God to rape him perverted. Since he read the bible literally, he could not go beyond the poet's plea to be ravished to what the poet wanted to convey by using such an image. And so she gave up. She could not allow him to defile what was holy to her.

And Jeremiah, on the other hand, couldn't understand her annoyance when he wanted to read the Bible to her while she was preparing dinner. He had decided he would start at *Genesis* and end with *Revelation*, and he estimated reading the entire Bible would take two years, and then he would start with *Genesis* again. The first evening he began to read to her, she turned on one of her classical records. He gave up.

Jeremiah grew to be an adequate lover, but he couldn't believe time spent enjoying sex was time well spent. There was just too much physical pleasure involved for him to feel at ease.

Only when his body was aching and weary from hard work or when he had done some good deed for someone else did he have a feeling of satisfaction. Spending hours as Sarah did, reading her poetry and novels, was an indulgent waste of time. He could never understand how she could take so much time for herself, time which benefitted no one.

The time of our lives should be spent as Christ spent his, in hard physical work as a carpenter, in helping those in need, and in spreading the good news of the Kingdom.

Sarah wouldn't accompany Jeremiah to church, and when he asked her to go with him, she would kiss him on the cheek and smile. "You have enough faith for the two of us. Say a prayer for me."

Jeremiah thought they would live a life of doing good together, but that had not happened. And yet he managed to transcend all their differences, many of which he blamed on himself, and he fashioned a life that was principled and noble.

And so it had been for the last fifty-two years, she living according to her beliefs, he according to his. Despite their differences, they loved and respected and honored one another just as they had promised when they married.

After the long years of being alone in his work and prayer, Jeremiah now had Naomi, and she had made all his disappointments become distant memories. She was like the coming of the Messiah, the fulfillment of an ages old promise. She was the light of his world. As Paul said, all things work together for good for those who love the Lord, and so they had.

Jehovah's Interlude

Life on earth is hard. Everyone in the area knew of Sarah's past. Her early sexual adventures, duly reported by some fellow teachers, were grist for the gossip mills of a small township. When she did decide to marry, she wanted a man who would ignore her past instead of reminding her of it during heated arguments. Once she met Jeremiah, she knew he was a magnanimous man, and so she chose him.

Isn't it strange the way some people meet one another and fall in love? You think they're on parallel tracks so their paths would never meet. Then someone throws a switch, and suddenly they're on the same track and destined to run into one another.

What was Jeremiah doing working on the stage crew at that play? He helped people all the time when they needed him and had no money to pay him, but building a set for a play was not his idea of helping the poor.

What prompted him to do it this one time? Why didn't he marry one of his own kind, someone from his church who was as single-minded about serving me as he was? Was he flattered that a woman as miraculously formed as Sarah would even speak to him? What was he thinking? But they met, and they learned to love one another.

All the hierarchy who run the administrative church on earth tell everyone the highest state a person can choose is to be a priest or a nun, to live a single life. But they're wrong.

The greatest gift I have to give a person is the gift of marriage, of loving someone and having someone love you. The couple may enjoy the love of children and they may enjoy the love of friends, but there's no comparison between what they share with children and friends and what they share with one another.

So I rejoice that Jeremiah and Sarah are together. I

know there's love between them, not a big, passionate flame like Sarah shared with Bill, but more than a spark. Perhaps a pilot light. Maybe that's the reason I'm putting my money on Jeremiah when Sarah arrives, and not Bill. Pilot lights burn all the time, twenty-four hours a day.

Once again, I ask for your prayers. Patrick of Ireland came to me and wants a parade up here on his feast day, March 17th, which isn't far away. He watched last year's parade in New York City, and when he saw the bagpipers and the kilts, the beautiful floats adorned with colleens, the policemen and firemen, and all the hard drinking Irishmen, he pleaded with me to let him organize a parade. I told him I didn't think there was enough money in the budget, but I'd try to come up with something. Next he'll want a float with himself chasing snakes all over it with his bishop's staff.

6.

"You old coot, what have you gone and done?" Sarah said as soon as Naomi and Jeremiah came in the front door. "Have you lost your mind? I'm going to have you locked up." Her usual composure was in disarray. She paced back and forth, her fingers running through her hair, her motions spastic.

Jeremiah leaned against the wall and began to take off his shoes. Naomi did the same. "I thought you'd have some hot cocoa ready for Naomi and me after being out in such a day."

"She should be locked up with you, following you everywhere like you were some sort of snake charmer. If she's around you much longer, she'll go crazy like you've gone crazy."

Jeremiah knew he'd be rebuffed if he tried to kiss Sarah. He walked over to Anna who sat at the table munching on some cabbage. He bent over to kiss her on her forehead. "Anna, how are things going?" Anna nodded her head in a positive manner so that she would not have to interrupt her eating. Naomi patted her mother on the shoulder. Once again her mother nodded in approval.

Anna felt pestered by their trying to get her attention, and she felt no guilt about her indifference. Her mother and father and daughter would have to make do on their own. What was getting on her nerves, though, was her mother's insistent pacing and shouting. She was used to her parents' quiet arguments and civilized disagreements, but she had never seen or heard her mother like this. It was going to have to stop. Anna was reaching her limit.

"What's the problem?" Jeremiah asked. "I'm going to make some hot cocoa for Naomi and me."

At that moment, the door opened with unusual vigor, and Millicent came in. Without seeing her brother-in-law, she began to weep and speak at the same time. "Did you hear what he's done? Six people have called me already to tell me about it until I had to take the receiver off the hook. We're disgraced. He's gone and ruined our family's name."

"What did they have to say, Millicent? I still can't figure out what you and Sarah are upset about. Now can't you both calm down and tell me what horrible thing I've done?" He turned his back again to pour the boiling water into two cups to make hot chocolate for him and Naomi.

Millicent didn't know what to say. She had vowed never to come into his house again while he was home, and here she was, caught like some intrusive mouse. She backed away and moved toward the door. "You tell him, Sarah. He's your husband," she said, grateful that her own husband had at least not brought her to this state of humiliation.

"Speak for yourself, Millicent," Jeremiah said. "Be not afraid," he said, lapsing as he often did into a biblical expression.

"You raised Bill Carroll from the dead! You shamed the whole family of Kingsfords," Millicent shouted, losing control of her emotions.

Jeremiah looked at both Sarah and Millicent in turn, and he felt sad, bowed down by the weight the Lord had seen fit to place on him. He took a cup of cocoa and gave it to Naomi, and then he sat down at the table with Anna, stroking her hair for just a moment as he sat.

"I had nothing to do with what happened to Bill. As a matter of fact, I tried to stop it from happening. Ask Naomi if you don't believe me."

"It's not grandpa's fault," Naomi said, sipping the hot cocoa. "The Lord made him do it. He wrestled grandpa to the ground right before we got to the Carroll's house, and he wouldn't let him up until grandpa gave in. Grandpa was thrashing about, trying to wrestle him right back, but the Lord was too strong for him."

"Do you expect us to believe that?" Sarah asked her

grand-daughter. "You follow him around all the time as if he's some kind of guru, listening to his nonsense, and now you believe everything he says. Perhaps my mind is failing, but I still have enough brains to know what's true and what's a fish tale."

"Sit down, Sarah, and you too, Millicent, and have a cup of tea, and I'll explain what I can," Jeremiah said. Millicent approached the table, but Sarah didn't answer him and kept pacing, talking to herself about madmen and what would happen to them when she drifted off forever.

Since Millicent had moved from the door and was standing near the table, she decided it would be less embarrassing if she sat down rather than retreat to the door. Jeremiah got up from the table, poured her a cup of tea, which she accepted with a bare nod of appreciation, and then he sat down again.

"As I said," Jeremiah began in a calm tone, "I had nothing to do with what happened. I was only the instrument of the Lord. The Lord said to me that I had to perform at least two miracles while I was alive for people to know I'm a saint.

"The Catholics, as I told Naomi, say the two miracles have to occur after the person's dead when someone prays to him or her for a miracle of healing. But Protestants don't make people saints, so the Lord said I have to do the miracles when I'm alive so they'll know I'm a saint and erect a statue of me. Don't you think I tried to resist? Don't you think I knew there'd be trouble?"

In a shrill, unnatural voice, Sarah said, "You should have told him, 'no'. You should have said, 'I'm just not doing it.' Instead you give in to what you say are his demands! Make some demands of your own," she wailed, her hands moving feverishly through her hair as if she were losing her mind.

"I tried. I can't. Don't you understand? I wrestled with Him, but I lost. And once I realized He was too strong for me, I had to follow His word." Jeremiah wanted Sarah to understand, and not be angry with him. He didn't want to upset her.

Sarah shook her head and sat down in dismay. "You knew how it would affect me Jeremiah. Why did you have to do it?"

"I don't have an answer. I don't have answers to a lot of things he does and did. I don't see how he got away with driving the money changers out of the temple when there were police all over the place who would have stopped him. But that's not the point now, is it?"

Jeremiah took a deep sip of his cocoa. He loved the buttery, chocolate taste, and he could feel not only his throat, but his stomach being warmed.

"You're a babbler," Sarah said. "You're like those people in your bible who tried to build the tower. You can't understand what anyone else is saying."

And Jeremiah went into a deep reverie, a silence where he could no longer hear anyone. He was at peace, sure of Naomi, the Lord, and himself. He had no sense of having performed a miracle on his own, for the Lord's was the power and the glory. And as he had been walking home from the Carroll's with Naomi, he heard the voice of the Lord whispering to him, "Well done, good and faithful servant."

That was all he wanted to be, a good and faithful servant. The rest was necessary to make a living and provide for his family, and he had done that. He had been both a provider and a servant. He was content, and he hummed a hymn to himself, "Amazing Grace."

Sarah stamped her foot. "Would you stop the humming and tell me what is the point of all this? Are you delusionary. Are you not paying attention."

"How do you explain," Naomi asked her grandmother, "that Grandpa raised Bill Carroll from the dead. I saw it myself. I saw him sit up, brush sleep from his eyes, and begin to talk. It was a miracle. No one can change that."

Sarah sighed, walked to the stove, and poured herself another cup of tea. It was the end of life as she knew it. It was the end of peace when she wanted peace so much, when she wanted the quiet which should come with her growing old. "You've gone and done it, Jeremiah. All the crazies will start bringing the blind and the crippled and the disturbed to our front door for you to cure them. We'll never know privacy again until our days are over."

"And those Catholics are going to say you're possessed by some kind of demon," Millicent said, "and it was through the power of the devil you raised Bill Carroll from the dead."

"That's what they accused Jesus of doing in chapter twelve of Matthew's gospel," Jeremiah said, "of casting out demons by the power of the devil. But Jesus told them it would make no sense for the devil to do that. 'If Satan casts out Satan, he is divided against himself; how then will his kingdom stand?'"

Anna grew angry and more angry as they argued. Where was the peace she had earned? Where was the god-given right she had to eat her food without people carrying on about some old miracle? Who cared whether Bill Carroll was alive or dead anyway?

Anna refused to tolerate what they were doing to her. She stood up and put her massive hands under the edge of the table and tipped it over. Since Millicent was sitting at the opposite end from Anna, the table landed on top of her as she fell backwards in her chair.

"Stop!" Anna shouted. "Stop your bickering. I won't have it. I deserve to eat in peace." She became spiteful in her anger. "Mom, I heard the talk around town when I was in high school, about you and Mister Carroll. The other kids said I got the best marks in Mister Carroll's class because you used to be his lover."

Sarah was crushed into silence.

"Millicent, are you all right?" Jeremiah asked as he

began to lift the table off her. "Give me a hand, Naomi." And the two of them managed to get the table off Millicent and back on its legs.

Anna wouldn't help them. She had said things to her mother that she had left unsaid for many years. Whatever small thread had held their relationship together was cut, but Anna felt purged of her frustrations in her moment of fury. It was time to make a change in her life.

Sarah looked at her daughter and grew pale. What was unsettling about life, she thought, was there was no end to the pain. In your old age when you thought you had suffered all the blows that could descend upon you and still survived, there were more to come. Life wouldn't be done with you until it had defeated you and you had conceded. She had reached the moment of concession.

"Aunt Millicent," Naomi said, "are you all right. Is anything broken?"

"I think I'm dying," Millicent said. "I think all my ribs are broken. One of the sharp edges of a rib might pierce my heart." She lay in disarray, the tea having spilled on her and stained her dress. She was so meticulous about her appearance that despite her fear, she was embarrassed.

"That's not going to happen, Millicent," Jeremiah said. "Don't get hysterical. We're going to call the ambulance."

"But everyone in the township will know," Millicent said. "What are we going to say happened? We musn't tell anyone that Anna tipped the table over on me." She began to cry in frustration.

"We'll tell them you fell backwards off your chair," Jeremiah said, "and that's the truth. Dial 911, Naomi, and ask them to send the ambulance."

"And tell them not to blow the siren," Millicent said. "It's bad enough the way things are without announcing to the world they're coming on an emergency, blowing that fool siren."

Jeremiah knelt down next to Millicent to see if he could see or feel any broken limbs or ribs. As he began to look for signs of a twisted leg or arm, and then to touch her chest to feel her ribs, Millicent became upset. She blushed.

"I don't want you laying your hands on me, Jeremiah. I don't want you performing any miracle on me like you did on Bill Carroll. Just let the doctors take care of me."

Jeremiah stroked her forehead and stood up. "I couldn't work any miracle on you, Millicent. You have to believe in the power of God coming through me before I can do anything."

"Well, I certainly don't believe that," Millicent said, pain beginning to seep through her voice.

"Then you have nothing to worry about," Jeremiah said.

"I reached them," Naomi said. "They'll be here soon."

"I'm going outside," Anna said, a miracle in itself that she would not only leave the house, but that she would tell them she was leaving. She opened the door and waddled out into the cold without a coat, but the many rippled layers of her flesh protected her.

Sarah sat down on a chair next to her sister's broken body. "I'm so sorry, Millicent. I never saw Anna like this. You know that. I upset her by my carrying on like I did."

"You were right to get upset, Sarah. I'm still upset myself. I can just hear the ambulance men talking about us when I'm strapped down in the cot. Can you come with me?" she pleaded. "I'm afraid."

"I'll go with you. Don't worry. I won't leave you until we find out if they're going to admit you to the hospital. I'm going over to your house and get some nightgowns, a robe, and slippers, just in case they keep you overnight."

"All right. The key is in my purse. But hurry back."

"I will. Try not to worry," Sarah said. She was sorry

for Millicent, but happy to be distracted at least for a time from her husband, the miracle worker, and her granddaughter, the witness.

The crowds came just as Sarah had predicted they would. Having packed the few things Millicent would need in case she had to stay in the hospital overnight, Sarah saw them as she walked across the street to her house. There were hundreds of them, some in cars, some on snowmobiles, some on cross country skis. The healthy out of curiosity; the sick out of hope. The unbelievers and the sceptics; the blind, the deaf, the lame.

Sarah was terrified. They looked like a mob advancing on her house, and she knew they wouldn't be satisfied until they had seen Jeremiah perform wondrous deeds, and if he did not appease them by miracles, who knew what they would do? She could feel violence in the air.

She was torn. Her place was with Jeremiah, but she had to take Millicent to the hospital. Why did he have to meddle in other people's lives and make hers so complicated? When she got back inside the house, she told Jeremiah about the crowd, trying not to show her panic because of Millicent and Naomi.

Jeremiah nodded his head, opened the door, and went out on his front lawn to wait for the crowds. As they got within a hundred yards of his house, Jeremiah began to take off his clothes. What little sun there had been during the fierce day was shrouded by cumbersome clouds, and the wind had brought the temperature to ten degrees below zero.

The crowd began to slow their pace as they saw Jeremiah disrobing, but they still kept coming, the reporters and cameramen in front. He had begun his day in the morning as if he were vesting himself for a religious ceremony, and now he began divesting himself of his cap, his three sweaters, his shirt, and his winter underwear until he was naked from his head to his waist.

Soon the crowd was all around him, the reporters

asking him questions about the miracle he had performed on Bill Carroll and why he was taking off his clothes. The cameramen, like voyeurs, were taking pictures of him as he disrobed. Without a word, he sat down in the snow, unlaced his boots, removed his socks, and then stood up.

"Are you crazy?" people shouted. When he didn't respond, they shouted again, "You're insane. You're going to freeze to death."

Jeremiah unloosened his belt buckle, pulled down his zipper, and slid out of his corduroy pants. All that remained was his long underwear, and he pulled it down and stepped out of it until he was naked. His skin was old and shriveled, his member and testicles shrunken from the cold, and his bones protruding as if they were elongated tumors.

"Don't you know there are women and children here, old man? Put your clothes on. You're embarrassing everybody."

Jeremiah stretched out his arms as if he were hanging on a cross. "Behold the man, your miracle worker," Jeremiah cried out, "a heap of skin and bones. I can perform no wonders unless the Lord works his power through me. See me in all my naked nothingness. See me for what I am, a powerless servant, an empty vessel of clay, the least of all His disciples."

The reporters stopped sticking their microphones in his face, the cameramen stopped taking pictures, and the crowd turned and went away, not only disappointed, but ashamed.

In the distance, one could hear faintly the sound of a siren.

Yahweh's Interlude

When the crowds used to hound my son to perform miracles for them, he often fled into the mountains or went out on Peter's boat to get away from them. But what about that Jeremiah! He takes his clothes off!

I never would have thought of that. He used himself as a symbol, an empty vessel, useless until someone pours something into it. Through his nakedness he showed the crowd he was powerless, yet in my eyes he is beloved because, like my Son, he is a suffering servant.

And when his time is fulfilled, because of his magnanimous spirit, I will command my messengers to bear him up and show him my salvation.

7.

Millicent was all right. She had a broken collar bone, but since doctors don't cast a collar bone, she left the hospital the next morning. They kept her overnight "just to be safe." She complained all the time about the pain, but that meant she was herself, so no one paid attention to her whining.

Anna, on the other hand, was not all right. She began to leave the house early in the morning and wander through the snow in the fields and the hills of the surrounding countryside. She had no warm clothes since she had never left the house. Sarah and Millicent had gone shopping and bought her a coat and a hat and some boots, but she refused to wear them.

The weather was less menacing when she was fat, but she began to lose weight so rapidly that each time she went out, the freezing temperature and the hostile wind tore into her and tortured her.

The snow in February was constant, and it became deeper and deeper in the fields and countryside. The winds were more fierce than the area had ever known, and they sent the temperature so low that the farmers were afraid for their livestock.

Jeremiah had to forsake his daily routine of helping all the widows who needed walks shoveled or snow brushed off the roof or pipes unfrozen in order to watch over Anna. Each day he got up early so Anna couldn't leave the house without his knowing it. When she did leave, he went with her. She never asked him, but she didn't refuse his company. She just ignored him.

Jeremiah was used to the cold and trudging through the dense snow, and except for his peaked cap, he was dressed for the weather. But he was almost eighty years old, and the daily routine which lasted for five or six hours each day was whittling away at him. He knew he had to be with Anna, even if she didn't speak to him, but he felt guilty about neglecting Naomi.

Naomi was confused and distraught by the sudden change in her mother, and she had only him to console her. Yet he was so tired at the end of their treks that he began to doze in his chair earlier and earlier, at the very times in the evening when he and Naomi used to talk.

Jeremiah wanted Naomi to come with Anna and him on the weekends or when she didn't have school, but even though she was a good walker and had learned to keep up with her grandfather, five and six hours were too much for her. She would fall down in the snow from weariness and weakness, and Jeremiah would have to take her home, leaving Anna alone, which he didn't want to do.

Anna ate little. She stood at the kitchen counter while the rest were at breakfast or dinner, picking at some lettuce, raw carrots, and broccoli. She was gone during lunch time, and so she ate nothing then. At least Sarah and Jeremiah were grateful that Anna drank water, not much, but enough they thought to keep her from becoming dehydrated. About once every ten days or so, she ate as if she were in a frenzy, but soon afterward they could hear her retching in the bathroom, having induced herself to vomit.

Jeremiah had no idea what had prompted her to stop eating, but then he had no idea what had prompted her to eat so much. He didn't think the incident about the miracle could be responsible for the change. It had to be something more than that.

Two months passed, and it was March 21st, the first day of spring, but the weather was still brutal. Anna set out for her walk at six o'clock in the morning, Jeremiah at her side. She had lost three hundred pounds, Jeremiah estimated, and there was little left of her body, perhaps ninety-five pounds. Her gait was slow and halting, and she began to fall every hundred feet or so. Jeremiah bent and lifted her to her feet each time, but his back began to ache so much that he could hardly stand.

"Anna, you have to be reasonable," Jeremiah said. "You can't keep trying to walk all day, and I can't pick you up much longer."

For the first time Anna began to notice that he was walking by her side. "You should go home, Dad," she said. "The weather's bad, and you'll catch cold." She sounded concerned, he thought. Hope began to rise in him.

"Anna, I won't leave you alone. I'm worried about you. What are you trying to do to yourself? You're going to die if you keep this up." Jeremiah was about to cry. He felt grief beyond measure when he thought of his only child's dying, although he was certain she had little interest in living. "Why are you doing this?" Jeremiah asked again. "Your mother and Naomi and I are so worried we can't sleep."

"I'm leaving, Dad."

"Leaving? Leaving where?" He was afraid she meant she was going to leave by starving herself to death.

"I'm leaving Mom and Naomi and you, and I'm going to start a new life. I'm tired. I'm tired of listening to Mom's poetry, and I'm tired of your preaching. I'm tired of aunt Millicent's complaining all the time, and I'm tired of Naomi's making me feel guilty. I'm moving away to some big city where no one will know my past or worry about my future."

"But how will you live? You're not well with all the weight you lost. How will you get a job in the condition you're in? I can give you some money, but I don't have a lot."

Jeremiah knew he was losing his child. "Cursed be the day on which I was born," he whispered to the Lord. "The day when my mother bore me; let it not be blessed. Cursed be the man who brought the news to my father, saying, 'A child is born to you, a son.' Let that man be like the cities that the Lord overthrew without pity; let him hear a cry in the morning and an alarm at noon, because he did not kill me in the womb; so my mother would have been my grave, and her womb forever great. Why did I come forth from the womb to see toil and sorrow, and spend my days in pain?"

"I'll survive, Dad. I'm going to start eating again, now that I've lost all that useless flesh. I'll get a job, some kind of job. I'm not worried. You'll take care of Naomi. She loves you more than anyone. She's the daughter you never had."

"But you're my daughter," Jeremiah said, "and I'll worry about you every day of my life."

"Today is the last day you'll have to worry, Dad," Anna said, a smile on her face. Then she collapsed in the snow.

Jeremiah knelt down beside her, and he lifted her arm to get a pulse, but he could feel nothing. After a few minutes had passed and she seemed to be slipping away from him, he pulled her arms up over his shoulders and bent until he had her body on his back, her arms reaching down the front of his overcoat. Then he tried to stand, but he couldn't get up.

"Lord," he cried, "hear your servant in his need. For I know my transgressions, and my sin is ever before me. Against you alone have I sinned, and done what is evil in your sight, so that you are justified in your sentence against me. But have mercy on me according to your steadfast love; according to your abundant mercy, blot out my transgressions.

"Lord, give me the strength of Samson. Help me save my daughter. Do not punish me for the sins I have committed against you. Hear me, O Lord, and have mercy on me according to the multitude of your great mercies. Bend your ear to me, and give me strength to lift her on my back."

Jeremiah tried once more, and he began to feel some power in his arthritic knees even though they throbbed with pain. He could hear the crackling of his joints as he lifted up his right knee. With his right elbow leaning on his knee for support, he began to raise himself, his back crumbled like the letter "C," but still holding on to Anna and pulling her farther up his back.

He had been a man of great strength when he was younger, and he could lift a sick calf on his shoulders and carry it for a mile. There was, however, little power left in his body now, just determination.

He struggled to balance Anna's weight on his back, but the weight of her body shifted to his left side and he fell into the hard-packed snow, Anna falling with him as though they were two figures in a sculpture. Jeremiah had struck his left side, and he felt a sharp pain in his shoulder. He knew it wasn't broken, just an old tendinitis, but spasms of pain flowed into his shoulder.

He hadn't let go of Anna's arms which he still held across his back, and so he began to stagger to his feet once again. No matter how hard he struggled, he couldn't move from that position, so he let Anna's arms drop lifelessly from his shoulder.

"Although our iniquities testify against us, act, O Lord, for your name's sake; our apostasies indeed are many, and we have sinned against you. O hope of Israel, its savior in time of trouble, why should you be like a stranger in the land, like a traveler turning aside for the night? Why should you be like someone confused, like a mighty warrior who cannot give help? Yet you, O Lord are in the midst of us, and we are called by your name; do not forsake us!"

Then he turned Anna over, her face looking up at him, and he tried to hold her under her arms and pull her as he walked backward through the snow. But he had to stoop too low and his back gave way, and once again, he collapsed, barely missing Anna as he fell.

His face hit a hard-pack, his nose and forehead crushing into the ice. After a moment, he could feel the wet blood on his forehead and see the blood gushing from his nose. He picked up snow in both his hands and applied it to his forehead with his left hand and his nose with his right hand. In a minute or so, the cold pack of snow had congealed the flow of blood.

In his frustration, he cried out on the world, but the area was desolate, and with the wind screaming, no one could hear him even if someone were around. As he sat there, gasping with deep breaths for oxygen to feed his body muscles, he could feel the cold air burn into his lungs with each breath. After a time, however, his body had absorbed enough oxygen so he could get onto his knees. He prayed.

"All my enemies are watching for me to stumble," Jeremiah prayed, "so that they might prevail against me and take revenge on me. But you, Oh Lord, are with me like a dread warrior; therefore, my persecutors will stumble and they will not prevail. Oh Lord of hosts, you test the righteous, as you are doing with me now, but with you at my side, I will succeed. Give me the power, Oh Lord, to lift this child of mine and bring her home."

Jeremiah heard a voice within him. "Jeremiah, my servant, pick up your child, put her over your back, and walk. You will bring her home, but not the way you have planned."

Jeremiah began to move toward Anna, and somehow, he found the strength to put his arms under her arms and stand her up. For a moment he hugged her loose body to him and wept, but then he turned around, holding onto one of her arms, and then grasping the other as he reached behind his back. Once again he pulled Anna onto his back.

He fell three more times, and the snow and ice on the ground ravaged his body, but he managed to rise, and when he thought he could no longer go on despite the strength given him by the Lord, he heard the roar of motors approaching. It was the sound of two snowmobiles, racing across the snow packed fields, criss-crossing one another's paths with daring maneuvers, until the drivers saw Jeremiah and Anna and drove toward them.

"What's the trouble, old man," one of the teenagers asked.

"My daughter's not well, and she collapsed in the snow. I'm trying to carry her home." He struggled to get up and lift her once again, but he fell down.

"You need help, old man. You can't carry her," the other boy said. 'We'll get you on our snowmobiles, one on each, and we'll bring you home."

"God bless you," Jeremiah said. "God bless you."

"We'll worry about being blessed later," the first boy said and laughed. "That's not high on the list of things we want."

They lifted Anna with ease and put her on one snowmobile, securing her as well as they could with their belts, and then Jeremiah got on the other. In a short time, the boys had brought them home.

"How can I ever thank you boys?"

"No problem, old man."

"What're your names?" Jeremiah asked.

The one boy laughed. "My name's Simon," he said. "My father gave me that crazy name. Like simple Simon was a pieman." He laughed again.

"My name's Judah," the other boy said. "We're brothers. My father gave us both weird names."

They got Anna off the snowmobile and carried her into the house.

"See you, old man," they said. "Stay home. The weather's too mean for someone your age." And they left, running back to their snowmobiles and heading out for more fun before it became dark. They had come in from New Jersey for the weekend with their snowmobiles, and they had wasted a lot of daylight helping those strangers.

Elohim's Interlude

You have to like Jeremiah. There he is, almost eighty, trudging through deep snow, enduring savage winds and whirling snow bruising his face, exhausted beyond endurance, unsure of what Anna is planning to do, and yet he goes on, my suffering servant. Like Daniel, he is greatly beloved. He would have given his life for Anna, and both of them would have died if Simon and Judah hadn't seen them and brought them to safety.

As he tried to lift Anna and bring her home, I felt the pain of my Son when they tortured him. He was led like a lamb to the slaughter, but why? Why did he have to suffer? I have never told anyone the reason. And I have chosen Jeremiah to suffer, and I have never told him the reason. There are some things beyond human comprehension.

I will continue to avoid John the Baptist; Jerome; that hypocritical, sin and sex obsessed Augustine; and a horde of other "canonized" saints who annoy me, but I will walk these streets with Jeremiah at my side, proud to call him not only my servant, but my friend.

I'm going to tell you a secret. Humans don't have a lot going for them. They can get bad genes which affect their moods, rotten parents who abuse them, and awful environments from which few are able to escape. They're subject to a million temptations which many of them can't resist: drugs, alcohol, money, sex, power, perversion, things that have the appearance of ripe fruit.

Having taken all these limitations into consideration when I created them, I decided they're all going to be up here with me after they leave earth. If I don't like them, I won't hang around with them, but they'll be happy.

The ones who were evil, like Hitler and Stalin and Ida Amin and Pol Pot and a gang of others, are not going to be tormented for all eternity in flames. They'll have to go through deep depression, anxiety, sleeplessness, and grief for a million years, but their suffering will come to an end at that time.

There is no hell, no forever and ever. When you read in *Matthew*, (that anti-semite, and himself a Jew), chapter 5, verse 30, about the whole body being thrown into hell, for which the Greek is gehenna, you have to understand that gehenna was a place outside of Jerusalem where they burned the town garbage. Matthew must have thought it was a good metaphor for punishment by fire.

What some of these zealots write about me smacks of the inquistion and witch hunts and torture and all those things evil fanatics do in my name. That may be the way humans treat one another, but I'm upset by anyone's thinking or writing that I would do that to those to whom I gave life and for whom my Son gave his own life. Predestination, the elect, everlasting fire, and all that nonsense are tales meant to scare gehenna out of my people, to keep them in line and prevent them from enjoying their lives. As that funny, crusty curmudgeon H. L. Mencken says to me every time I run into him, "A puritan is someone who's afraid that somewhere in the world someone is enjoying himself."

8.

Anna began to eat, moderately, things that would give her strength, and she gained about ten pounds in a month. When she weighed 105 pounds, she felt stronger, and she left one day when no one was home. There was a note thanking her father for the hundred dollars he had given her several weeks before, and telling them she was going to New York City and would contact them when she felt whole. She didn't know when that might be.

Sarah often thought of a line from Frost's poem, "The Death of the Hired Man," that spoke to Anna's presence. "Home is the place, where, when you go, they have to take you in." Poetry had kept Sarah's world intact, but now guilt swept over her. She had been unnerved for twelve years by Anna's silent presence, but at least she knew Anna was safe at home. Now there would be no end to her worry nor her guilt from the moment Anna blamed Sarah for the humiliation she suffered at school.

Sarah's life reminded her of a Greek tragedy. She had felt no guilt in her sin of fornication, but the gods must have been offended for they continued to lavish punishment on her for it.

Nothing had worked well for Sarah except her poetry, and she had leaned on its wisdom to keep her world from falling into chaos. Now even poetry seemed of little use, and with Anna's leaving, there were no more chances for Sarah to right her life, to keep it from tipping over. She tried to think of something to stabilize her feelings, but she could think of nothing. She knew it would be hypocritcal to turn to God in her hour of sorrow since she had never bothered with him before.

She was adrift, a sailboat without a rudder nor a sail, adrift in uncharted waters, listing from one side to the other, heading toward a whirlpool. She began to fear for her sanity.

She had been the rationalist, the devotee of the Enlightenment, the high priestess of poetry, certain that her refinement and intellect would lead her to a confident superiority as she negotiated the labyrinth of life.

Now she felt herself in the maze which confined the Minotaur, through which only Theseus could thread his way to slay the monster. She knew she should be a presence and a comfort for Naomi, but she kept running into an intricate network of blind passages as she sought an exit from confusion. Her feet had no firm footing as she tried to escape the monster.

She had not realized Anna had known about her time with Bill. Sarah had strayed with joy into the arms of her lover before Anna was even born, and she had never thought that such old gossip would arise again to cause Anna to be the victim of her classmates's taunts.

But years later when Anna had Bill as a teacher, mothers must have told their children about the old scandal. In Anna's outburst of anger, perhaps even hatred, Sarah had become aware that her affair had painful consequences for her daughter. The sins of the mother had been visited on the daughter.

People say it's never too late to heal, but Sarah knew that wasn't true. There are cuts and bruises and gashes that never develop scabs and fall away. She knew her affair had left open sores, and none of the many lines of poetry she had committed to memory could close one of them.

Her favorite figure of speech was irony. She had taught her students that what one expected to happen and what did happen was the basic plot for all great works of literature. The Greeks based their drama on a character's excessive pride in thinking he was superior and the consequent disaster that befell him because of his arrogant choices. "The irony of it all," she would say to them.

And now it had happened to her. Her belief in poetry and in romance as superior to everything else in life, as that for which one should sacrifice everything, had exposed her folly. Yet, despite the folly and the pain she had caused, she knew she would have done it all over again.

The memory of having known Bill Carroll in every physical, intellectual, and aesthetic way had nourished her throughout her life. Choosing not to have had him would have been impossible. Without him there would be as Frost wrote "nothing to look backward on with pride." Pride was the wrong word for illicit sex, perhaps, but in an ironic sense, it was hubris, excessive pride, that had caused her downfall.

She had thought she could live life free from any moral restraints, and she did, with seeming impunity. She thought that spirits like Bill and she had the right to disdain common people and their common morals. What she discovered, however, was that commoners meted out punishment for violating their moral standards, even on an innocent young girl like Anna.

She no longer had a choice to do other than she had done. The deed had been consummated, and the "scarlet letter" had been refurbished.

As she sat alone in the kitchen, she began to wonder if Millicent had been to see her. She knew Millicent visited each day, but she couldn't remember if she had been there that day. She laughed, a wry smile spreading over her face. Perhaps she was getting Alzheimer's. All the articles she had read said that it wasn't the long term memory, but the short term memory that was affected.

Maybe it was a good thing. Maybe Alzheimer's was her salvation. She might lose her memory, but with it she would lose the memory of present pain, even of past pain. She would drift along, narcotized by confusion as neurotransmitters failed and vaporized her mind.

She would dwell, not in this house nor this town, not with the notoriety that Jeremiah had brought upon them, not with the knowledge that Bill Carroll lived, not with guilt for Anna, but like a new born baby, with no memory of the pain of birth, of the danger of being born, of the consequences attendant upon life. She would revert to the time of the womb and the amniotic fluid that bathed her, and she would be unreachable.

It was a soothing thought. Others said it was their greatest nightmare, to lose their sense of themselves, to lose their awareness of those they loved. Yet Sarah thought they were wrong, that to be lost and unaware would be a balm.

Not knowing whether Millicent had been there that morning was a consolation. Perhaps it was a harbinger of things to come. She would have a cup of tea. She would wait and see what good things might happen to her memory if she were patient. She would wait and see if Millicent came barging through her door.

God's Interlude

People have to understand that I can't be responsible for everyone's happiness or unhappiness. If you're human, like my son was human, you're going to suffer. There's no way to avoid that. On the other hand, once you accept that fact, a lot depends on your attitude, on how you cope with the things that happen to you.

Sarah wants to drift into alzheimer's so she can avoid life's suffering and pain! With all her disdain for Jeremiah's way of life, she could learn something from the way he handles troubled times. Jeremiah never had it easy, and yet, he wakes each morning eager to do things for others, trusting in me to support him no matter what happens. The trouble with Sarah is that she's the center of her world, and when her world begins to collapse, she starts running for the darkest shelter.

Jeremiah is just like my David. He's not one of those sissy saints the pope makes sometimes. He's human, with all his faults and all his failings, and yet they leave no blemish because he loves people and forgives them and watches over them. Before he dies, he'll even forgive old Jonathan Kingsford.

Some of the saints the popes make drive me mad. Take the "Little Flower" (what a nick-name!) who is so sweet that she makes me nauseous. Her "little way of holiness" is oleaginous, so I put her in charge of listening to "sweet-prayers." She still annoys me with her habit of passing out roses on the street corners everyday, telling everyone, "God loves you." I do, of course, but as I said before, that doesn't mean "God likes you." She's never been on my dinner list.

Last week she asked me if I could have her fitted with wings so that she could drop roses everywhere up here. I wonder who she thinks is going to clean up all the petals.

As the cliche goes on earth, I said, "get a life," not out loud, of course, or she'd cry until I apologized, so I just smiled and ignored her.

When the popes "make saints" like the "Little Flower," they must think I'm a pansy. If they're going to "make saints," then give me saints like Mary Magdalen who was a better apostle than my son's apostles, the wimps, running and hiding while the three Mary's were standing with my son while he was on the cross. You can depend on tough saints like those three. They were loyal to the end.

And next on my wish list, I want a statue of my servant Jeremiah to be erected in or near the town square, and one way or another, I'll get my way.

Time has passed for the people in my novel, and it is now a year since Anna left. The spring has broken early after another bad winter, and the weather is delightful But my beautiful Sarah's mind is slipping away. She remembers some things clearly while others have faded from her memory.

9.

Jeremiah was confident all his pain would work together for good because he loved God. That's what Paul said, and he believed everything Paul said. He had fallen with Anna in the snow, but the Lord had rescued them from the wrath of nature. The Lord had not saved Anna only to let her lie down in bleak night. There was a purpose to what He had done for her, and Anna would be all right. It might take a long, long time, but she would be fine.

While Anna needed him, he was with her everyday, and he had to forsake those others in need, for his first duty of love was to Anna. Since she had left, he prayed for her each night and morning, but he got on with his works of mercy. As Paul said, the love of Christ compelled him.

"Sarah," Jeremiah asked, "will you be all right while Naomi and I are gone? We won't be too long. I've got to check on old Mister O'Brien. He probably needs a lot of things fixed after the winter."

"You'll be going through town?" she asked.

"That's the fastest way to get to his house," Jeremiah said.

"What day is today?" she asked.

"It's Sunday. I went to church this morning. Don't you remember?"

"Of course I do," she replied. "What time is it?"

Jeremiah loved to take out his pocket watch because Naomi had given it to him as a present for Christmas. "It's about eleven-fifteen," he said.

"Is today Easter?" she asked.

"No. Today's Palm Sunday. It's a marvelous, warm day in April," he said.

"April is the cruelest month," she answered.

"Where did you get that from?" he asked, exhausted

by her depressive remarks since Anna had left.

"It's the opening line of *The Waste Land,* a poem by T.S. Eliot."

"Didn't you tell me once that man moved to England?"

"Yes, I did."

"No wonder he said that. The weather's always miserable in England."

"The weather's not his point."

"Then what's his point?"

"His point is that April, which should be a joyous time and a messenger of spring, brings us false promises. Spring is filled with emptiness."

"Sarah," Jeremiah sighed, "you've been so depressed since Anna left. Why do you want to read things like that? Some of your poetry must be happy."

"Oh, yes, some of it is."

"Then you should read that kind."

"Perhaps, I will," Sarah said. "So you're going into town on Easter Sunday?"

"It's Palm Sunday. Like I said, it's the easiest way to get to Johnny O'Brien's house."

"The Catholics used to have a big procession on Palm Sunday. St. Peter's Church. That's the name of it, I think. They'll be lots of them there," Sarah said.

"I know that," Jeremiah said. "What's the matter with going to town when they're having their procession?"

"Suppose they see you?"

"Suppose they do?"

"Didn't you tell me they chased you out of the Carroll's house? I thought you told me that. They haven't seen you in a long time."

"Yes they have, Sarah. They came out to our house expecting me to cure them that same day. Don't you remember?"

"Some people came out. What did you say they wanted? I don't remember."

"They wanted me to cure them."

"Cure them of what?"

"Of illnesses they had."

"And how could you do that?"

"I couldn't."

Naomi was listening as they talked, and she was filled with fear. Her grandmother seemed so distant, her voice drained of emotion, her mind sluggish but accurate on some things, clogged on others. It was like listening to an echo which was growing faint amidst the mountains.

Yet what she said sounded like the prophecies Naomi had been reading about in the Bible. In the tone of her voice there was a foreboding of evil that would befall Naomi and her grandfather. Even though the day was warm, Naomi felt a chill.

"Maybe I better stay here with grandma," Naomi said to her grandfather. "I can help her around the house."

"That sounds like a good idea," Jeremiah said. "I won't be gone too long."

"I don't want her to stay with me," Sarah said. "You might need her. I want her to go with you." She gestured with her hand as if waving both of them out the door. "Does Millicent live nearby."

"Just across the street."

"Ask her to come over. I haven't seen her in a long time."

"That sounds like a good idea," Jeremiah said. "Naomi, tell Millicent I'm going into town, and she'll come over right away."

"All right," Naomi said. "I'll get her."

"I'm going to make you a cup of tea before I go,"

Jeremiah said.

"That would be nice," Sarah replied.

Jeremiah turned his back to her, put a kettle on the stove, and turned the burner on. Tears came to his eyes, and so he concentrated on the kettle rather than sitting down next to Sarah. How was Sarah's condition going to work together for good?

He would have liked to take her in his arms and tell her that everything would be all right, but he knew she would neither let him nor believe him. Even in bed where she often welcomed his strong arms about her as she lay with her back to him, she now grew restless when he touched her and often got out of bed and wandered about the house.

Since Anna had left, Sarah's mind had begun to dissolve, not dramatically, but incessantly. There was never any question in Jeremiah's mind about putting her in some institution. She knew who they were, and she never wandered away from home.

He knew he had "married up," but he believed their marriage had been happy. The vast dichotomy between their worlds was much greater than he ever could have imagined, but for all that, no one could have loved her and still loved her as he did.

Bill had refused to marry Sarah because of his family. Jeremiah would have forsaken everyone to marry her, everyone except his God. His love knew only that one boundary, and his one disappointment had been that he expected Sarah would consider his way of life holy since he lived in the service of God, but she didn't care about his God.

God was a part of her world as long as God remembered his place, but once Jeremiah began to preach to her about God's knowing our every movement and directing our daily life, Sarah became annoyed.

"With all the evil in world, with all the murderous wars, with Hitler's holocaust, and Stalin's starving his own people," Sarah had said to him, "what kind of God is it that you believe is watching over us? Some kind of sadist?"

The more he tried to convince her of God's love, the more she argued with him, until one day, he gave up. Sarah was not ready, he decided, to embrace the will of God and the love of God. Each day he prayed for her conversion, never losing hope that God, as Paul said, who began his work in her, would bring it to fruition.

The tea kettle began to whistle. Jeremiah wiped the tears from his eyes with the sleeve of his shirt, and poured Sarah's tea. As he put the cup in front of her, he asked, "Would you like some cream?"

"Please. And some sugar."

"The sugar's on the table. Right in front of you."

"Oh. I see it. Yes."

Then Millicent opened the door in her brusque way, Naomi trailing behind her.

"Millicent, would you like a cup of tea?" Jeremiah asked.

"I'll pour one myself," she said, not wanting to prolong his presence. "You and Naomi can go now, on your errands to the Catholics."

"We try to help everyone," Naomi said. "Grandpa's not prejudiced."

"I'm sure he's not," Millicent said, a touch of sarcasm in her voice. "Now go along, the two of you." She was emboldened by their need for her to sit with Sarah.

"Bundle up," Sarah said.

"It's a beautiful spring day, Grandma," Naomi said. "All we need is a sweater."

"I told you how nice it was out," Jeremiah said. "Remember, I was out earlier when I went to Sunday services."

"Of course I remember," Sarah said, peeved that he felt the need to remind her.

Jeremiah and Naomi put on their sweaters. As they left, Jeremiah said, "Don't worry. We won't be gone long."

"Stay as long as you want," Millicent said, glad to have her sister to herself. She had a story to tell her that Sarah was never going to believe.

"Sarah," Millicent said as she poured a cup of tea, "You're not going to believe this story. It's crazy, but it's true. I know you won't believe me," she said again as she sat at the table, "but I swear every word is fact."

"I can't wait to hear it," Sarah said, and she tried to keep her mind from closing.

"Do you remember the night Anna tipped the table on me and I had to go to the hospital? Of course, you do, you went with me in the ambulance."

"Of course I did," Sarah said.

"Yes, well, I thought maybe one of my ribs was about to puncture my heart. Anyway, the doctor made me stay over night, and the next morning, before the doctor discharged me, this volunteer worker came into my room to see if there was anything I needed. He was a distinguished looking older man, tall, silver hair, strong features, a wonderful smile, his own teeth."

"I don't remember your telling me anything about that," Sarah said. She wondered if even her long term memory was being erased.

"Well, I didn't think much of it at the time, except I thought he was too forward." Millicent began to blush. "Sarah," she said in a whisper as if there were someone in the house to overhear her, "he came over to the bed and held my hand while he was talking to me. And then he began to rub my hand and my arm, almost up to my shoulder, and he said, 'Millicent, you have the most beautiful eyes, and I could look in them forever.' I couldn't believe it. Sarah, you and I both know my eyes are a nondescript brown, but he kept staring at them until I had to look away from him."

"Were you afraid? Did you get his name?" Sarah

wondered if she would remember his name after Millicent told her.

"He told me his name was Matthew Arnold, a retired professor of English Literature at the University of Michigan, and he said he had traced his heritage back to the great Victorian poet Matthew Arnold. And I said to him, 'that's hard to believe,' and he said, 'I have the genealogy to prove it, and I'd like to show it to you.'"

"Isn't that wonderful? Matthew Arnold is one of my favorite poets," Sarah said.

"He asked me if he could come out to my house and show me the genealogy. Well, I thought he had a lot of nerve, and so I told him "no." I said, "I hardly know you.""

"I never saw him again, until last month when I was at the market to buy some apples to make a pie. He tipped his hat, and asked me again if he could come out to my house and show me the genealogy. He was such a good-looking man, and seemed so interesting, and so interested in me, that......"

"Did you tell him where you live?" Sarah asked.

"I did, Sarah. I haven't felt this way since I was a young girl in high school," Millicent said. "I invited him out to dinner tonight. I'm so excited. A cultured man. Nothing at all like William Burnside. Matthew Arnold is not an ordinary man."

"Isn't it dangerous to let a stranger into your home?" Sarah struggled, trying to decipher if her life was over and Millicent's was beginning.

"He's not really a stranger," Millicent said. "I've been meeting him for lunch several times a week. I didn't want to tell you in case he turned out to be something bad, like a pervert."

"Did he?" Sarah asked.

"No, of course not. He's a gentleman. He holds my hand a lot. Sometimes it's hard to eat because he doesn't want to let go. I think I'd marry him if he asked me. Don't discourage me, Sarah. Please don't. He's the first ray of light in my life for years. Please don't tell me not to do it. I need your approval. I've been very lonesome."

"I'm happy for you, Millicent." Sarah reached over and touched her hand. "I'm just worried."

"It's worth a little worrying to me," Millicent said.

Of course it is, Sarah thought. Of course. As she was forgetting to remember, Sarah tried to recall her trysts with Bill. Sarah thought memories of romance might help Millicent as they had her, but she couldn't remember how old Millicent was, and whether age made a difference, or if Bill was still alive.

"You deserve the poet Matthew Arnold, Millicent. Now tell me again, where did you say you met him? At church?"

With all kindness and tenderness, Millicent told the story to Sarah several times without breaking into tears. Matthew Arnold had come into her life when she most needed someone, a time when she was losing her beloved sister to darkness.

God's Interlude

It's never too late. There's someone out there for everyone. Writers and school teachers make fun of cliches like these because they display a lack of imagination, but they're often true. As unbelievable as it was that Sarah and Jeremiah met at the play and got married, it was serendipitous that Anna upended the table on top of Millicent and that the doctor kept her overnight in the hospital where she met Matthew.

As late as our life might be in years, it's a blessing to find someone to love us, to watch over us, to be concerned about us. Even as old as I am, and I'm older than quarks, I want people to love me.

I was lonely, (I'm a person too, you know) and one day I thought, wouldn't it be nice to have people created in my image and likeness so they could love me and I could love them back? And so I decided to do it.

It took hundreds of millions of years, but in my time, that's no time. And now I have a lot of friends, like my servant Jeremiah. And you know what? It was worth it, including the ones who drive me crazy. They're still worth loving, each and everyone of them. And even if I don't like some of them and try to avoid them, they have friends who like them and that makes them happy.

So let's raise a glass to Millicent. She's eighty years old, and she's willing to take a shot at happiness. She told Matthew she's only seventy-one, and she's eighty; and he told her he's related to the poet Matthew Arnold, and he's not. But he likes to touch and he likes to feel, and he says wonderful things about her eyes, and she loves being the subject of his poem. And he likes being idolized, and she feels blessed to have him to idolize.

They'll be happy, and I'll be happy because she'll only have eyes for Matthew when she gets here, and I won't have to listen to her chirping. William will be happy because she won't remember him, and he can live out eternity in peace. As they say on earth, it's a no lose situation, or do they say win/win? As kids say, whatever.

10.

Jeremiah and Naomi set out for Mr. O'Brien's house. The distance to Carbon was about two miles, and then another quarter mile to O'Brien's. Jeremiah figured it shouldn't take them more than fifty minutes.

Only a few months ago, Jeremiah could have made it in forty minutes, but the long winter walks with Anna through the snow and ice had made the arthritis in his knees and his back flare. He also had begun to have pains in his legs from his knees down to his feet, and since he avoided going to a doctor, he had no idea what was causing them. Even at night when he lay in bed, the pain shot through his legs and wakened him.

He began to think dark night was fast closing in on him, but he banished the thought from his mind. Thinking that way was too much like the sin of despair. The only cause he could think of was that the Lord had afflicted him with "a sting of the flesh," as Paul said, perhaps to keep him humble lest he begin to think he had raised Bill Carroll from the dead through his own power. Whatever the reason, Jeremiah knew there would be no relief from his pain. As Paul said, "I carry the marks of Jesus branded on my body." He would suffer with the Lord.

"I know, O Lord," Jeremiah prayed, "that the way of human beings is not in their control, that mortals as they walk cannot direct their steps. Correct me, O Lord, but in just measure; not in your anger, or you will bring me to nothing."

"Jeremiah," the Lord answered. "My strength is sufficient for you."

The day was so filled with glory that Jeremiah began to shiver with joy. The Lord was bringing him into a state of rapture where he would be taken up to the heavens. It had happened to him before when something of awful moment was going to take place.

"Naomi," Jeremiah said, "I'm going into a 'state.' Let's sing a hymn of praise to the Lord. As Paul said, 'this is the day the Lord has made. Let us rejoice and be glad.'"

Naomi was afraid when her grandfather went into a "state." Something scary was going to happen like the day he raised Mister Carroll from the dead. The Lord would seize her grandfather, and the Lord would wrestle him to the ground and pin him.

Naomi knew she could do nothing to help him. She was not yet chosen. Someday she hoped she would find favor with the Lord, but it would happen only if the Lord extended his grace to her as he had done with her grandfather. Nothing she could do would make it happen. Nothing she could do would stop it from happening.

"Look at the crocuses, Naomi. No matter how harsh winter is, nothing can prevent them from sticking their heads above ground. They're like the power of God. They just burst in on us. And see those forsythia over there! They're the first yellow bushes of spring, like yellow ribbons 'round the oak trees."

"And the sun, grandpa. It's starting to warm me. People say it's bad for your skin, but there's nothing like the sun. I could sit in it all day long."

"Naomi, let's sing psalm 96. We both know that one by heart. We'll praise the Lord because's it spring, and it's Palm Sunday, the day of Christ's triumphal procession into Jerusalem, and the Sunday before the great feast of the Resurrection. You start, Naomi. I'm always off key."

As they walked along, Naomi began to sing with a voice that sounded like a skylark, that soared without effort from one register to another, in the most pure tones Jeremiah had ever heard. He could picture her in eight or nine years, an evangelist in a long white dress, leading her followers in singing praises to the Lord. Just her singing would bring them to a confession of faith in the Lord Jesus Christ and to immersion in the waters of Baptism. Jeremiah joined Naomi in singing, a baritone voice filled with gravel, but rich with joy.

> "O, sing to the Lord a new song;
> sing to the Lord, all the earth.
> Sing to the Lord, bless his name,
> tell of his salvation from day
> to day. Let the heavens be glad,
> and let the earth rejoice; let the
> sea roar, and all that fills it; let
> the field exult, and everything
> in it. Then shall all the trees of
> the forest sing for joy before
> the Lord."

As they sang, Jeremiah could feel the Spirit come upon him, and he lost his place on earth and was lifted into the heavens. He could no longer feel the heat of the sun nor see the colors of the earth.

In rapture he was taken into the core of the sun, but he felt no heat. Then rain began to collapse on him, thunder battered his ears, and bolts of lightning snapped at his feet. Whirlwinds encircled him and threatened to engulf him. Jeremiah trembled, but he was unharmed.

He felt the space he stood on give way beneath his feet, and he was suspended in air, looking down on earth. He saw raucous winds agitate the heavens and lightning crease the sky, its bolts crackling as they clawed from the clouds. The lightning singed the hair of the trees and seared their branches which clung to them in desperation. Nature was menacing, and yet it seemed threatened itself, striking out like some terrified horse trapped in a barn fire. Then silence fell.

Jeremiah saw an open hall, and at the end of it there was a throne so bright that he could not look at it for more than a few moments. There were angelic creatures surrounding the throne, their wings covering their faces as if they were afraid to look upon whoever sat on the throne. And in front there were angels whose swords were drawn and pointed in Jeremiah's direction to keep him from approaching.

A voice as if deep within a volcano ruptured the silence. Jeremiah knew the voice was from the one who sat unseen upon the throne. Jeremiah hugged himself in dread, and he prostrated himself even though he was at an infinite distance from the throne.

"Be not afraid, Jeremiah. You have found favor in my sight. I have extended my grace to you, and I have invested you with the power of the miracle worker. I have chosen you as my beloved servant, but you must suffer, for suffering saves, and there is much in the world that needs saving. I have set a task for you this very day. Place your trust in me, and you will not falter. Go now, Jeremiah, and say nothing of this to anyone, except Naomi."

Jeremiah began to fall from the core of the sun, through the heavens, yet there was no fear in his flight. Rather there was a feeling of being supported by the palm of someone's hand and of being set gently on the earth. After several minutes, he became aware of the conscious earth, and he could hear the plaintive sounds of Naomi as he lay on the ground.

"Grandpa," she cried as she shook him with tenderness, "are you all right? Do you want me to run to that farmhouse over there and ask them to call an ambulance? You look so pale, like a picture of one of those horsemen in the book of Revelation."

Jeremiah began to stand up, and Naomi helped him to his feet. He brushed himself off as if he had fallen in a hay pile. "I was terrified, Naomi, but I'm fine now. The Lord swept me up, and I heard his voice speaking to me, telling me that I had found favor in his sight."

"What did He look like?" Naomi asked, realizing she would have to write every bit of it down in her journal. She was sure this would be the most exciting chapter of all, and it had to be so real that people would have to believe.

"I never saw the face of Yahweh. Not even Moses was allowed to see the face of Yahweh. 'You cannot see my face; for no one shall see me and live,' Yahweh said to Moses. I could make out his throne, burnishing like the glint of gold, and I heard his voice, and I could see the angels surrounding his throne, covering their faces with their wings like they were afraid to gaze on His countenance. And there were warrior angels, standing with their spears or swords drawn to keep me from approaching the throne."

"Were you afraid?" Naomi asked, writing everything down as fast as she could. It was hard work being her grandfather's evangelist. If any of his words or deeds, and especially his moments of ecstasy weren't recorded, it would be her fault. Sometimes she thought it was too much for her, but she knew he didn't have anyone else to do it. She felt the Lord was giving her these tasks before He decided whether or not He would make her one of His chosen.

"I was," Jeremiah said. "It's a fearsome thing to be caught up in the hands of the living God. Even though you know He loves you, it scares you as if you were going to die and no longer be a part of everyone's life and just disappear from your home and all the places you've known for so many years.

"And when you hear his voice like Moses did on Mount Sinai, your feet tremble and the ground shakes and you're in an earthquake. And yet," Jeremiah said, "even though you're terrified, you know you're safe, and you know you're loved. But lest anyone forget, Yahweh is infinite power."

Naomi wrote as much as she could, but then Jeremiah stood up and began to walk. "Come on Naomi, we've just begun the day, and there's a lot of things to do before our work is done."

They set out for the small town of Carbon where the township had a small building to conduct its affairs. There wasn't a meeting of the township supervisors until Thursday night, but Jeremiah would be there and present them with the will of the Lord, that they erect a statue in the town square in memory of his having followed in the paths of the Lord and performed a miracle by the grace of the Lord. He had missed many meetings because he had to protect Anna, and he stayed home with Sarah on evenings when she was bad. But this Thursday would be the day of reckoning. It had been a long time in coming.

As they came into town, the Catholics were coming out of St. Peter's church, holding palms in their hands, and lining up to take part in a procession back into the church to commemorate Christ's triumphal entry into Jerusalem.

They were dressed up in their finery much as they would be on Easter Sunday, the girls and women with colorful hats and dresses, and the men in suits which lasted for years since they wore them only on special Sundays. Father Minihan was greeting his parishioners, and since the warm day was so welcome after the wretched winter, everyone was happy and talkative.

Jeremiah stood across the street watching them. He loved ritual and symbol, something which the Baptist church didn't have enough of, and he loved the ceremony of Palm Sunday. Once he had even slipped into the back of St. Peter's to watch the Easter Vigil Service. When all the lights were out and the people were holding lighted candles to celebrate the light of Christ coming out of darkness to illuminate the world, Jeremiah was moved to tears. Despite all their shortcomings, the Catholics had a liturgy that appealed to Jeremiah.

As he and Naomi waited for the procession to begin, Mary Carroll, who was with her husband, Bill, and her two boys, Kevin and Conor, who had assaulted Jeremiah at the wake, saw them watching.

"What are you staring at?" She hollered at them. "Be on your way. You've caused enough trouble, you devil worshippers."

Bill Carroll turned around and saw them. He waved to them and began to walk across the street to greet them. He had sent Jeremiah a note thanking him, but he had never seen him to thank him in person.

"Where do you think you're going?" Mary asked, her hand grabbing the elbow of his suit coat. "You're not going over to those Protestants," she began to scream. "I won't have it. And on Palm Sunday! They're here to make fun of our procession."

The two months left on her husband's term life insurance policy had expired, and now she'd get nothing when he died the second time. She had argued with the insurance company that she had a signed death certificate with the state of Pennsylvania seal on it and they had to honor it and give her the money, but they had refused.

She had some grand spending plans when he died, thinking of how she could afford a nice cruise which Bill would never take her on, cheap a person as he was. Despite his obsession with being "frugal" as he liked to call it, they had little extra money. She suspected that he was hiding some of his school pension money from her, but if he was, she was never able to prove it. When she saw Jeremiah, she boiled up inside herself, thinking how much she hated him for cheating her out of all that money.

Because Bill was so mortified by his wife, he backed down from her wrath and turned his back to concentrate on the procession. But his two sons, Kevin and Conor, ever protective of their mother, began to bellow at Jeremiah and Naomi.

"Get moving, or we'll speed you along," Kevin shouted. "You've no business here."

"You're a son of the devil," Conor yelled, "and your

miracles are the work of the devil."

All the Catholics were now staring at Jeremiah and Naomi. They wished they would leave, because they knew what awful tempers the Carroll brothers had. They had caused trouble in the community since they were boys.

Naomi tried to pull her grandfather away and go to Mr. O'Brien's, but she couldn't budge him. He seemed to be locked in a trance as if he couldn't hear their threats.

"Grandpa, come on," she pleaded. "We have to get out of here. They're going to hurt us if we don't. Please, grandpa, please." Jeremiah paid no attention because he couldn't hear her.

Father Minihan, the pastor, walked over to the Carrolls. He was old, but he never backed away from trying to set things right that were going wrong, even though he was far past his days of strength.

"Mary, Kevin, and Conor, will you please calm down? Just ignore them. Jeremiah and Naomi are doing no harm. They mean no disrespect. Come now. I want to begin the procession. Get in line with the others. Let Naomi and Jeremiah be."

There had been a crew in front of the church for the past week, replacing a water line that had ruptured, and there were a lot of stones lying about from the broken pavement. Both Kevin and Conor picked up stones, and they hurled them at Naomi and Jeremiah. One of the stones missed Jeremiah by a few inches, but one stone hit Naomi in her left temple.

Everyone was frozen like a tableau as Naomi sank to the ground in slow motion, startled as if she couldn't believe what had happened to her. As Jeremiah, now conscious of the world, watched, she crumbled to the ground, her neck arching backward, her arms flung out to her sides, and her legs splayed as if she were trying to make a snow angel. She was staring up into the heavens, her eyes glazed in unbelief.

Jeremiah felt the loss of innocence weigh on him like

the weight of the globe. Evil had been unleashed on her whom he loved best, and evil had overpowered the goodness of Naomi. Blackness enveloped her figure, and the triumph of Palm Sunday had yielded to the defeat of Good Friday. The cross had overwhelmed the crown. The palm was a hollow symbol.

Kevin and Conor Carroll ran away to the parking lot and jumped into their pickup truck. They gunned the motor and fled.

Doctor Eiden broke through the crowd to Naomi's side, shouting for someone to call an ambulance. When he knelt beside her and grasped her arm, feeling for a pulse in her radial artery, he found none, for life had slipped away from her in the onslaught of hatred.

With his fingers he searched for a pulse in her right carotid artery, but there was none. The most the ambulance could do was take her to the hospital to await an autopsy by the county coroner. He shook his head, stood up, patted Jeremiah on the back, and walked away. Too many times life had slipped through his fingers.

There was nothing Father Minihan could do. Neither Jeremiah nor Naomi believed in the last rites as a sacrament. He managed to bend on one knee and recite a silent prayer for the soul of Naomi, blessing her as he stood up. Jeremiah never looked at him. All he could see was astonishment in the face of Naomi as if she had been deflowered by evil.

The Catholics stood stricken. They had never taken to Protestants, nor Protestants to them, but they were stunned and saddened at the brutal hatred inflicted on such a young child. They couldn't take their eyes from her fallen body, and tears came in repentance for what two of their own kind had done to blacken their religion.

Jeremiah stared at the face of Naomi, thinking of how the Lord had brought him to the ultimate test of his faith. "Now you've taken everything from me, Lord," he said in a whisper. "My wife, my daughter, my grand-daughter. Now I have nothing left.

"But I was like a gentle lamb led to the slaughter. And I did not know it was against me that they devised schemes, saying, 'Let us destroy the tree with its fruit, let us cut him off from the land of the living, so that his name will no longer be remembered.' Why does the way of the guilty prosper? Why do all who are treacherous thrive? You plant them, and they take root; they grow and bring forth fruit. But you, O Lord of hosts, who judge righteously, who try the heart and the mind, let me see your salvation, for to you have I committed my cause."

And darkness settled over the whole town, a darkness that could be felt, and the people were afraid. They could no longer see the fallen figure of Naomi except in shadow. The great figure of Jeremiah rose and stood in silhouette and lifted up his arms as if he were reaching beyond the earth, his neck stretching backward as he turned his face upward. He began to pray, and everyone was able to hear what he said.

"Oh Lord, empower your servant. Death and evil have only the appearance of victory, while yours is the kingdom and the power and the glory, forever and ever."

Then Jeremiah knelt down, and he spread himself on top of Naomi's body, and he groaned in spirit as if he were willing life into her. After a time, he knelt again, and grasping the hand of Naomi, he said, "Talitha cum," which means in Aramaic, "Little girl, get up." And Naomi got up, and she began to walk, and the people were overcome with fear. A ray of light, like a spot on a stage, split the darkness and lit up Naomi and Jeremiah as they embraced one another in awe and wonder at the mighty deeds of the Lord.

Allah's Interlude

Why do my people hate one another? Protestants? Catholics? Jews? Muslims? Black? White? Yellow? Why do they persecute and enslave and abuse someone who is not like them? Why do they want to hurt a young child like Naomi, a girl as pure of heart and spirit as you can find in the world?

What harm would it do if you let everyone else lead his or her own life in peace? If someone doesn't believe in the things you believe in, so what? I'm not looking for crusaders to fight battles in my name. Believe me, I can take care of myself. I never wanted anyone to hurt another person in my name. What a perversion of my intentions, people taunting, belittling, and even killing other people in the name of me!

The only thing I ever wanted from people is that they love one another. That's the best way of loving me. Did you ever notice that's how Jeremiah lives his life, loving those around him, even Millicent who drives him crazy with her nose in the air, disdainful of those without a pedigree.

If you ever harm another person or hate another person because they don't pray to me or believe in me the way you think they should, don't use me as a reason for the evil you do. Listen to me, and listen to me good. I want you to know, once and forever, the only thing I look for is that you love one another, no matter what your race or color or religion is.

Don't tell me that people who have a certain belief don't know the truth and it's up to you to convert them to the truth. It isn't. It's up to you to be tolerant and to mind your own business. As Robert Frost wrote in his wonderful poem, "Good-Bye, and Keep Cold," 'something has to be left to God.'

Set an example by your lives, not by your mouths.

Francis of Assisi preached by example, and he was someone I really liked while he was on earth. Spend your life as Francis spent his life, loving everyone and everything.

Up here, however, he drives me nuts. He spends all his time looking for birds, stretching out his arms and expecting them to land on his hands. I know a lot of you love birds, but I don't allow birds up here. I used to, but they started dumping all over my people because there are no statues up here, and so they dropped their droppings on anyone who stood still for more than a second. Francis won't give up though. From morning till night he warbles his bird calls.

Remember: love one another and don't lose your sense of humor.

11.

Jeremiah took Naomi's hand and continued on to Mr. O'Brien's house. The sun was shining, and the breeze was warm. There was no danger in the air.

"Grandpa, what happened to me? All I remember is getting hit in the head by a stone. Did I fall down? Was I unconscious? Why do I feel fine, like I wasn't hurt at all? There's not even a lump on my head."

Jeremiah bowed his head and went into a deep reverie for several minutes. As usual Naomi did the same, but this time she was agitated. She wanted to know what had happened. It was the first time she ever thought of interrupting his thoughts. She was ready to complain when he lifted his head.

"You were dead, Naomi, killed by one of the Carroll boys. Doctor Minihan checked your pulse. You had none. The ambulance would have taken you to the morgue, but the Lord raised you up."

Naomi could not believe what her grandfather had said. She could not imagine herself dead. In all her short life, she had never thought of her own death, not one time. She felt safe with her grandfather, as if he had been appointed by God to watch over her and only her.

"He raised me up? How did He do it? Did you do it, grandpa?"

"I didn't do it. The Lord did it. He used me like He did with Bill. Listen to me, Naomi, and never forget what I'm going to tell you."

Naomi took her hand from his and began to reach for her pencil and note cards.

"There's no need for that now," Jeremiah said. "You can write what I'm going to say in your diary when we get home. I think you'll remember everything.

"You're beloved of the Lord, Naomi. I told you that before, but today the Lord put me to the test, whether I truly believed, kind of like Abraham when Yahweh told him to sacrifice Isaac, the child of the promise.

"When you pleaded with me to walk away from St. Peter's church, I tried, but I couldn't lift my feet. I knew what was going to happen to you when I saw those Carroll boys, but I couldn't stop it.

"But the Lord taught me a lesson. No one can harm you, Naomi, because you're part of His plan."

"What plan, grandpa?"

"I don't know, Naomi. I don't know."

They walked down the road to Mr. O'Brien's house, both of them silent within their own thoughts, Naomi taking her grandfather's hand again and holding it tight, knowing she was holding the hand of a saint.

Jeremiah was worried about what he would find when he got to the house. He hadn't seen Mr. O'Brien in two months, and he knew no neighbor would have looked in on him.

He was a paranoid old man, about eighty-nine years old, and no one had ever liked him. He had owned his own butcher shop, and since he sold only the highest quality meat and was the best butcher in the area, he had done a good business. But he had never been friendly with his customers. His wife had died about fifteen years ago, and they had no children.

The only people he allowed in the house were the ones who delivered his food, and, of course, he complained to them about their cuts of meat. He could have had people from several agencies come into his home and help him, but he was afraid they might have power to put him in a nursing home which would use up his money in a short time. So he refused, telling Jeremiah, "Johnson ruined the country with all his damn social programs."

O'Brien had given Jeremiah a key to his house. He

didn't believe a thing Jeremiah said about religion and faith, but he trusted him. When something went wrong in the house, Jeremiah would fix it. Even though O'Brien had no one to leave his money to, he took advantage of Jeremiah's willingness to help him without pay.

As Naomi and Jeremiah came up on the front porch, he could smell decomposing flesh, and when he opened the door, he knew O'Brien had been dead for awhile. Naomi began to gag.

"If you want to go outside, Naomi, I'll understand," Jeremiah said. "His body must be ripe, and the smell will lead me right to him. The Lord knows what he looks like."

"I'm your disciple, Grandpa. I have to be there so I can write about what you're going to do."

"O. K. Follow me. I think the odor is coming from the second floor."

Jeremiah felt guilty about Mr. O'Brien. He had assumed responsibility for watching over him, and he had failed him. Sarah had absorbed a lot of his days and nights lately, and he had had no time for O'Brien.

There was a long winding stairway leading up to the second floor. All the floors were solid plank oak, and the stairway was a magnificent walnut. When Mr. O'Brien's wife Mollie was alive, she polished the floors and stairway for hours each day. She loved the pungent smell of the lemon oil as it soaked into the wood.

The house was stately, although few people were allowed past the kitchen. Jeremiah had been there many times over the years, fixing one thing or another for Mr. O'Brien. Even at that time the old man had hated to part with money, and so he paid Jeremiah with his wonderful cuts of meat. Once his wife died, however, the old man lost interest in maintaining the sumptuous house. He asked Jeremiah to take care of only the necessities.

As Jeremiah reached the top of the stairs, he knew Mr. O'Brien had died in his room or in the bathroom. The stale odor of decomposing flesh, baked blood, and feces had captured the air. Naomi began to gag again.

"Naomi, breathe through your mouth and not your nose. It will help a bit."

Jeremiah glanced in the bathroom, but he knew the old man had died in his bedroom. "If you have to throw up, Naomi, throw up in the bathroom toilet. Then take some water to rinse the vomit away. Do you have any mints with you?"

"I have some gum."

"Don't use it now. Save it until after you throw up."

Jeremiah went to Mr. O'Brien's bedroom. The door was closed, and he opened it and walked inside. There is no stench like decomposing flesh. It smells like meat gone bad when you forget to refrigerate it and leave it out for several days. No smell, however, bothered Jeremiah. He had worked in a slaughter-house when he was a teenager and never threw up. It was a gift, he supposed, like a person who never gets seasick has a gift.

Mr. O'Brien was lying face up in the bed, his eyes open as if he had been startled when death arrived. He had on his pajamas that were full of feces because the sphincter muscle had relaxed when he died.

Mr. O'Brien's death had to be reported to the coroner and no one was supposed to touch or move the body, but Jeremiah decided to wash him and clean him of his shame before prying eyes invaded his lack of dignity. He knew it was illegal, but he believed his act of love was more important than the law.

He went to the linen closet, took out some towels, a pail that was sitting on the floor of the closet, and a large plastic waste bag to put all the sheets and towels in. He filled the pail with water from the bathroom, went back to the room, took the pajamas off Mr. O'Brien, and began to wipe him clean of the feces that had hardened on his body. Some of the flesh came off with the towels because he had to scrub the body to get the feces off, but he had expected that. Skin always slipped away when a person had been dead for a long time.

After a few minutes, Naomi ran into the bathroom and threw up.

It was an hour before Jeremiah had finished washing Mr. O'Brien. He put a clean pair of pajamas on him, changed the bed, disposed of the sheets and towels in the garbage bag, and called the coroner. While he was preparing the body, Jeremiah thought of Joseph of Arimathea, taking the body of Jesus from the cross and wrapping it in a clean linen cloth for burial.

The Lord's Interlude

I was looking down at Orient beach on the French side of St. Martin Island one day, a beach where nudity is optional, and there were a few handsome people, both men and women, in the buff. It was a joy to see them in their young, glorious bodies, taut and tight and firm, the way I meant them to be in their early years.

But there were old nudists too, who were wrinkled and aged and boney and droopy and pendulous. The law of gravity seemed to be pulling them downward to the sand. They were happy, but they were not a sight you'd like to look at every day, or even once a year.

When I gazed back on the young ones, I thought of lines from the English poet Ernest Dowson, "they are not long, the days of wine and roses." Bodies grow old and decrepit, and all the "lifts" available aren't going to stop their running down to death as the body seeks its road to incontinence, diapers, deafness, Alzheimer's, diabetes, arthritis, hormone-depletion, and lack of motor skills. It's the human condition. As they fall into the last stages of life and their naked bodies are not erotic to anyone, good people take care of them.

And so I decided to add to the list of the eight beatitudes since the readers of my first book liked them so much:

1. Blessed are those who care for the incontinent, who wipe them and change them; and afterward kiss them and caress them to let them know they are loved and that ministering to them was not unpleasant; for all of these are welcome at my table;

2. Blessed are those who care for Alzheimer victims, who are patient when they are ready to scream in frustration; who answer the same questions over and over; who keep themselves sane by laughing at times, without diminishing the person who suffers; for all of these shall share my house;

3. Blessed are those who assist the feeble when their arthritis flares, when their gait is halted, when they can no longer dress themselves, when everything is an effort; for all of these shall walk with me;

4. Blessed is my servant Jeremiah and all those like him who will not allow the dead to suffer indignity, who will wash them and change their clothes and make them presentable for the moment the funeral director or coroner comes to take their body away; for he and they shall be my friends all the days of their eternal life.

12.

It was August, and it was hot, and the heat warmed Jeremiah and eased the pain in his joints. He and Naomi had been out in their vegetable plot for an hour, pulling weeds, picking corn, potatoes, tomatoes, and cucumbers which they would have for supper with meatloaf, Jeremiah's favorite meal.

They had left Sarah on the front porch in a rocking chair, bathing in the sun, and every so often they checked on her. When they came back toward the house, however, she was not there, and so they presumed she had gone inside.

As they entered the kitchen, they saw Sarah had taken the ground sirloin out of the refrigerator and put it in a large bowl. She stood beside it, not knowing what she should do next, and she was growing agitated. Naomi went to the refrigerator, took out a piece of bread, an egg, an onion, a garlic clove, and a bottle of barbecue sauce. Then she got a cutting board and a kitchen knife, and put everything on the counter for her grandmother.

Sarah smiled, and picked up the knife. She looked at all the ingredients, and couldn't decide what to do with them. Naomi put an onion on the cutting board. Sarah tried to cut the onion before removing the concentric outer leaves, but she couldn't get the knife to cut. Before Naomi could take the onion and remove the leaves, Sarah grew angry and threw the knife on the floor.

There was a knock at the door, and Jeremiah went to answer it. An attractive young woman stood outside the screen door, her hair cut short, the lower part curling into her chin. She was tan, and she wore a trace of mascara which made her eyes look very large and attractive. She wore a simple summer blue dress, and she smiled. Jeremiah looked at her for a moment before he realized who it was.

"Anna," he said softly as he opened the door.

"Anna." He opened his arms, and she walked into their wide expanse and embraced him. Then he held her away from him. "Anna, you look real fine."

Then Anna walked over to Naomi. She held out both her hands, palms up, and Naomi, shocked as if she were seeing an apparition, held back for several moments, and then took Anna's hands. "I'm so sorry, Naomi. I can't ask you to forget what I've done to you, but someday, you may be able to forgive me."

Naomi shook her head as if to agree, but she said nothing. This couldn't be her mother, she kept telling herself, this young attractive woman, but she knew it was. She told herself not to hope her mother had come back to stay with her, healed of her sickness. She told herself to believe her mother would leave again.

Then Anna turned to her mother, who was staring at her as if she were afraid. When Anna came near her, Sarah backed up and raised her left arm as if to ward off a blow. Anna turned to Jeremiah, waiting for him to explain what had happened to her mother.

"Your mother's left us, Anna," Jeremiah said. "We've not been able to reach her. She's been no trouble. Sometimes she wanders about the house at night, but she doesn't try to go outside. She's simply left us for some other place."

Anna looked startled. This bright, beautiful, well-spoken woman, blessed with a superior mind, had retreated from the world? "It was my fault, wasn't it?" Anna said. "When I flew into a rage and heaped guilt on her and began that manic walking and weight loss and left without a word, she decided she couldn't bear it. That was it, wasn't it Dad?"

Anna began to tremble, and Jeremiah took her in his arms again. "It's no one's fault, Anna, not yours nor Naomi's nor mine. We can do the very best we can for people or, sometimes, we can hurt them, but in the final reckoning, it's up to each one of us to hold ourselves together.

"And furthermore, the doctor says your mother has Alzheimer's, and there's nothing to be done about it. And neither you, my lovely Anna, nor anyone else can cause this wretched disease nor cure it." Jeremiah paused.

Anna stepped out of her father's embrace. "What are you making, Naomi? May I help?"

"Gramma was trying to make meatloaf. She couldn't remember how," Naomi said.

"I worked in a nursing home as an aide while I was in New York. There were people there who had memory problems. There were things they used to do to help them. Do we have any of those index cards your grandma used to use for her recipes?"

"I think they're in her desk. I'll look. Here they are. There's a whole pack of them."

"Is there a ballpoint pen there and some scotch tape?"

"Yes."

"May I have them, please? Thank you. Gramma is afraid of me since I'm a stranger to her, so you bring her over to the kitchen counter."

While Naomi was trying to lead her grandmother over to the counter, Anna took the meat out of the bowl and put it on a plate. She began writing in big letters on the cards: ONION, MEAT, GARLIC, SAUCE, EGG, BREAD, and then she scotch-taped each card next to the ingredient.

Sarah was still resisting Naomi's gentle entreaties, and Anna kept writing on the cards and taping them: STOVE, OVEN, REFRIGERATOR, SINK, DISHES, BOWL, TABLE, CHAIR, COUCH, LAMP, DESK, PEN, until she had marked at least twenty or twenty-five things.

Sarah became curious and went to the kitchen counter to see what Anna was doing. She looked at the card and the ingredient, but she showed no sign of connecting them. She said nothing.

"Watch mom," Anna said, "I'm going to pick-up the

meat," and she lifted the ground sirloin in one hand and the card in the other, and she showed her mother both of them, and put the meat in the bowl. Then she took the onion.

"Naomi, hold the card in front of Gramma while I cut the onion." Anna sliced off both ends of the onion and the sides to get rid of the outer layers. Then she put the onion on the cutting board and began to dice it. She did the same thing with the garlic, and Sarah seemed interested in what she was doing.

After a few minutes, however, Sarah walked away, picking up the cards on the tables, the couch, the chairs, and letting them fall to the floor. Anna and Naomi watched her for a time, and then Anna continued to add the egg, bits of bread, and barbecue sauce. She mixed all the ingredients together, and molded them into an oblong shape for baking. Then she garnished the meatloaf with parsley. Anna grieved, but she didn't cry. It was too late for tears.

"It looks like a fine meatloaf," Jeremiah said, "as good as your mother used to make." Jeremiah came over to the stove. "Let's have a cup of tea, and you can tell us what you've been doing," Jeremiah said, putting the kettle on the stove. "Naomi, come over and sit with us, and bring your grandma." Somewhere in the depths of her mind, Sarah knew that she loved tea, and if they poured her a cup, she would sit with them and drink it.

They sat down, and when the tea was ready, Jeremiah poured each one a cup. "Anna, tell us a story. It seems to me it would be interesting to all of us."

Naomi looked at her mother for a moment, then dropped her eyes when she met Anna's gaze. She poured cream and sugar into her grandmother's cup, then stirred it for her. Sarah seemed calmer as she bent over the warm tea and sipped it, her head close to the cup all the time. Her regal posture and majestic demeanor which had singled her out as she sat at table were memories only in the minds of other people.

"When I took the bus to New York City, I sat with Maggie, a girl from Scranton, who was going to New York to find work. She was a lot younger than I was, but she had been to New York many times before she decided to move there permanently.

"She asked me where I was going to stay, and of course, I had no idea. So she said to me, 'why don't you come with me to the Gramercy Park area, around 19th street off Third Avenue on the East Side? There's a rooming house there just for women, and you'll feel safe until you find out where you want to live.'"

Naomi was still hesitant to ask questions. She kept glancing at her mother from time to time, but just for a moment, and she had a difficult time convincing herself that this young, stylish, attractive, well-groomed, big-city woman was her mother.

She was pleasant and kind and sensitive. It was no mother she had ever known in her life, and she was convinced this new mother was just a stranger who would walk out the door after they had supper, never to be seen again.

"Tell us more," Jeremiah said. "How was the place, and how did you get a job in the nursing home?"

"The place was fine, very clean and very safe. They had very strict rules about men visitors, but that didn't bother me. I wasn't in that frame of mind.

"The next day, Maggie showed me this ad in the paper for a nurse's aide at a nursing home, and so I went and applied. I didn't need any training for the job, and they asked me to start the next day they were so short of help. So I did, and it worked out well."

"Now for the big question, Anna," Jeremiah said. "How did you transform yourself to become this sophisticated, polished New Yorker?"

Anna laughed, a delighted, shoulder shaking laugh they had never heard before, and Naomi and Jeremiah were taken back, and even Sarah looked up to see what may have caused such an outburst. "I'm sorry. You never heard me laugh, and I've startled you. I laugh a lot lately. I think laughing is the sound of being well, and I laugh every day. I'm so happy when I get out of bed in the morning I hug myself."

Naomi moved her chair closer to her mother. She began to feel that things might be all right, that she might have a mother, at last, and she wondered if she too would begin to hug herself each morning.

"I'll always be the country girl floundering around in the big city, kind of like Eliza Doolittle in My Fair Lady. I have to admit I love New York. It's exciting, and even if you don't have much money, there's a lot of things to do. Maggie showed me how to have fun on almost nothing."

"You're going back there," Naomi said, a statement more than a question.

"I hope not," Anna said. "I was lost when I went there, and now, more than likely because of your grandfather's wearing out heaven with his prayers, I'm found.

"And there was another man, a minister, who used to come into the nursing home, sometimes late at night when everyone was sleeping. He asked to be called when one of his parishioners was dying so he could sit and pray with them.

"Often it was one of my patients he came to see, and he noticed I was depressed. He talked to me many nights about forgiveness and love and responsibility. What it came down to, really, he told me, was I had to get outside of myself, to think of others, and to do for others. If I did that, he said, my life would stop revolving around myself and I would get better."

"Where are you going to go then?" Naomi asked, still afraid to believe her mother would stay with her.

"This is still my home, I hope," Anna said, looking to Jeremiah for confirmation. With a great smile, he nodded.

"I'm going to stay here and take some classes at the College in Scranton to get my nursing degree. I found what I want to do in life is serve those who need me most. And I can serve better if I become a nurse. And when I'm not at school, I'm going to help with your grandmother."

Naomi moved her chair closer to her mother. "You're really going to stay? You mean that?"

"I need a daughter if you need a mother," Anna said.

"Oh, yes," Naomi said, "I need a mother more than anything else in the world."

Both of them got out of their chairs and held one another in the tightest of embraces for the longest of times.

"I can't change the past, Naomi, but you and I, we have a future together. I don't know anything about mothering, so you'll have to teach me as we go along." Anna kissed Naomi on the side of her face, a soft, tender, lingering kiss.

"You're learning real quick," Naomi said. "Just keep it up, and you'll do fine."

Yahweh's Interlude

With the large exception of Sarah's sliding further and further into an unkind world, the Bowman's had a happy house which was filled with laughter when Anna and Naomi were telling each other stories and jokes. Anna had to go to class three days a week, but the rest of the time she devoted to her mother.

Sarah was wearing underpants for incontinence, and Anna changed her and cleaned her four or five times a day. It was impossible to get her into the bathtub because Sarah was afraid of stepping up to get into the tub and then sitting down in the water. She fought Anna and Naomi so vigorously over the tub that all Anna could give her were sponge baths.

When Naomi and Anna were in school, Jeremiah stayed with Sarah. She sat in a rocker most of the day, looking out the window, watching the leaves fall. Jeremiah brewed her tea and fixed her lunch, using an apron as a bib so that she wouldn't get food over her dress.

Jeremiah took her collected poems of Emily Dickinson off the shelf, (they were all published now) and read each one of the 1775 poems to her. He read them slowly, and although many of them eluded his understanding, others he thought were interesting. Once in a great while Sarah would smile as he read a poem and take his hand, but he never knew whether it was because of the poem or some far distant memory.

As the sun was rushing through the window one day, Jeremiah paused in his reading, thinking how heaven might be this way: holding Sarah's hand, immersed in sunlight, reading her beloved poetry, all time in abeyance. If they could have lived their lives like this, alone, together, the two of them, he would have thought himself the happiest of men. But, he had been chosen.

When Jeremiah had to go to the bank or to get some

groceries, Millicent and Matthew would come to sit with her. Matthew loved to read to Sarah, and he would bring his own anthology of English poetry, and read the poems in an eloquent voice and with dramatic flair.

"Sarah, I'm going to read you Matthew Arnold's most famous poem, "Dover Beach," so concentrate," Matthew would say. Then in his deep baritone voice, which echoed like the roaring of the sea, he would dramatize the reading like an actor on stage, especially when he reached the last stanza. It wasn't a poem celebrating joy, but it was a great poem he knew Sarah would enjoy if she could.

> Ah, love, let us be true
> To one another! for the world, which seems
> To lie before us like a land of dreams,
> So various, so beautiful, so new,
> Hath really neither joy, nor love, nor light,
> Nor certitude, nor peace, nor help for pain;
> And we are here as on a darkling plain
> Swept with confused alarms of struggle and flight,
> Where ignorant armies clash by night.

Millicent sat with them, mourning her lost sister, and adoring her Matthew who had proven to be the kindest and most distinguished man she had ever known. And since Matthew Arnold had married her, she had to believe her present joy was a miracle.

When Millicent saw how tenderly Jeremiah cared for her sister, she set aside all her hostility toward him and even grew to admire him because he was true to every word he ever preached.

For a time I infused the home of Jeremiah with happiness that few people know. But I'm going to take Jeremiah to myself soon. His problems with breathing are due to congestive heart failure, and since he has avoided the doctor because of caring for everyone else, his lungs are filling with fluid, his heart muscle isn't strong enough to pump off the fluid, and soon he will fall into my arms.

But for the present time, no man could be as happy as Jeremiah. As I told you in the beginning of the book, I chose him to be one of my suffering servants like Moses, Ezekiel, Isaiah, and Daniel. My servants suffered, but not in vain. As I wrote about them in *Isaiah* 53, they will have their reward.

"Yet it was the will of the Lord to crush him with pain. When you make his life an offering for sin, he shall see his offspring, and shall prolong his days; through him the will of the Lord shall prosper. Out of his anguish he shall see light; he shall find satisfaction through his knowledge. The righteous one, my servant, shall make many righteous, and he shall bear their iniquities. Therefore I will allot him a portion with the great, and he shall divide the spoil with the strong; because he poured out himself to death, and was numbered with the transgressors; yet he bore the sin of many, and made intercession for the transgressors."

I'm happy to see everyone happy, but life can't just mark time. Anna has to become a strong daughter and mother, and Naomi has to strike out on her own without Jeremiah guiding her each step of the way. Anna has come full circle to the way of love, and she'll be strength enough for her daughter. Naomi will blossom, and she will do great things in my service, and I will enjoy the company of Jeremiah as he walks and talks with me. Except for David, there is no one so close to my heart.

By the way, I was talking to John the Baptist the other day. I try to avoid him, as I told you, but he cornered me, and with that deep, sonorous voice he begged me to listen to him. He wants me to give him a franchise to make deep fried locusts dipped in hot honey. He's convinced he'll make a fortune and says he'll cut me in on the profits, 50-50.

You think you have problems on earth, and you do, but try dealing with some of these saints. I told him I'd think it over, but not to get his hopes up.

13.

It was now the end of September, and the Board of Supervisors was having its first meeting after a recess in the month of August.

"Are you going to ask the Board of Supervisors to put a statue of you in the Town Square at the meeting?" Naomi asked. "If you do, people are going to think you're crazy, Grandpa," Naomi said, knowing she should try to stop him, and yet hoping he'd do it. The kids in her class wouldn't believe it! Two miracles and now a memorial statue!

Those kids never had any stories to tell about their grandparents. They were either dead or in nursing homes or sweet old people who baked cookies for them or sat in front of their television sets all day long, living life doped up. Her grandfather was alive and vibrant, living life with passion, and helping as many people as he could.

"You and I will lay it in their laps at the meeting," he said, annoyed that he was having a hard time breathing and had to slow his pace.

When he sat with Sarah, he was comfortable, but anytime he went outside to rake the leaves or cut the grass he'd find himself breathing through his mouth to get more air. And his feet were swelling. He was able to elevate them when he was home, but as soon as he walked or exercised, the swelling would come back. It was annoying.

"I'm worried about you being at the meeting, Naomi. I'll be a laughingstock. Even though it'll be in the name of the Lord I ask them to erect a statue, they'll mock me and try to put me away, or they'll throw me down a well, or put me in stocks."

"I've gone with you everywhere, grandpa. You're not going to get rid of me now because they might be nasty," Naomi said.

"They ought to agree for the sake of every single person in the township," Jeremiah said.

"Mr. Healey's on the Board of Supervisors, and he doesn't like you a bit, Grandpa. His daughter Franny's in my class at school, and she told me he thinks you're a looney." Naomi looked sideways to see how her grandfather would react. He changed more colors than a chameleon when he was angry, and it made her giggle till she could barely talk. Naomi noticed she was becoming more silly now that her mother was home.

"John Healey won his seat on the Board of Supervisors because he's related to everyone," Jeremiah fumed. "His mother and father had fourteen children, and not a blasted one of them ever left the township. The Irish are thick, Naomi. Look at the way they treated us at the corpse house.

"Mary Carroll isn't a bad sort, but that whole lot of dumb Irish put her up to acting like that. When you get one of them alone," he said, "they're fine, but put them together, especially at an Irish wake with all their drinking, and they can be meaner than a bull in heat."

"Franny Healey and the other Irish girls don't like me. They call me 'that Protestant,'" Naomi said.

"Some insults are best forgotten, Naomi, and best forgiven. Remember that. A person can carry pain and bear up under almost anything, but hate and spite are just too heavy a load."

Jeremiah Bowman trudged along, silent and thinking, meditating on the 'why of things' as he had explained his pensive moods to Naomi. They never lasted a long time, but four or five times a day, he'd plunge deep in thought or deep in prayer, searching for the wisdom of the Lord, plumbing the depth of his heart to see what was true and what was good.

Since he had decided the township should erect an appropriate memorial in honor of his life of holiness, a voice within him kept repeating the phrase of Solomon from the book of *Ecclesiastes*, "Vanity of vanities, and all things are vanity," and he questioned whether his intentions were pure or just vainglorious.

But another voice whispered that a graceful song should be sung forever, and the song of his life was filled with grace. Then he would hear the words of Matthew's gospel, "You are the light of the world. No one, after lighting a lamp, puts it under a bushel basket, but on the lampstand, and it gives light to all in the house. In the same way, let your light shine before others, so that they may see your good works and give glory to your Father in heaven."

And those words sustained him. The memorial was the light of his good works in the world, and it was not for his own glory, but for the glory of the Father in heaven. The Board of Supervisors had to understand that. He would make them understand, for the light of the Lord and the power of the Lord would shine through him.

"Suppose the whole board says 'no,'" Naomi asked when he lifted his head. "What will you do then? If they're all against you, how can you get it done?"

Naomi knew he did what he said he'd do, but that was when it depended on himself to do the doing. Now there would be other people involved. John Healey and Ned Oates and Peter McNally were all on the Board of Supervisors, and not one of them liked her grandpa.

Peter McNally was married to Mary Carroll's sister, and John Healey walked across the street when he saw Jeremiah because John swore the old man was possessed. The best of the three was Ned Oates. He was a thinker, and he kept his emotions under control.

When they turned her grandfather down, she hoped they wouldn't be mean to him. He was the best person she had ever known, and she didn't want anyone to hurt him. No matter what she had done in her whole life, he had never scolded her. He had only one rule which he said was from the book of the prophet Micah: "Do justice, love kindness, and walk humbly before your God."

"Naomi." he said, as if he were about to deliver a sermon, "I wouldn't give the least little speck of time to thinking about the supervisors. Those three gentlemen have a part to play, just as you and I have, in the meeting. Just a part, that's all. 'Unless the Lord build the house, they labor in vain who build it.' They might think they have power, but they're just instruments in the hands of God. Yahweh is Lord of the heavens and of the earth, and his will, not their wills, will be done.

"Just look at what the Lord did when he raised up you and Bill Carroll through me. Why, Ned and Peter and John are just small men in the Lord's drama, and in light of those miracles, they should do what's right."

"What part do I have, grandpa?" she asked. "I'll bet they won't even let me in if it's crowded. That Mr. Sanders at the door will say, 'since you're not old enough to vote, you have no right to be here.' I won't even get to hear what goes on."

"You're not only my disciple, Naomi, but my evangelist too. You have to be there, right next to me. You see, Naomi," he said, speaking softly even though there was no one else around, "what I have in mind is for you to give testimony that I've done all the good things I claim I've done. You've been with me a whole lot of time except when you're in that blamed school, and you've been witness to most of the good deeds I've done. It's only been the last five years since you reached the age of reason that you can swear to what I've done, but there's no one that's been as close to me as you."

"Yeah, but I've only been alive a short time compared to you, grandpa," she protested, half afraid and half delighted she was going to be the most important person at the meeting of the Board of Supervisors. "Grammy and you have been living together for fifty-two years, and she'd know every good thing you ever did. She should be the one, if she could remember. Not me. I'm just a young girl."

"All the great prophets said the same thing you're saying, Naomi. When God asked them to testify for him, they all had excuses. Jeremiah said: 'Ah, Lord God! Truly, I do not know how to speak, for I am only a boy.' Isaiah said, 'Woe is me! I am lost, for I am a man of unclean lips.' And even Moses, the greatest of all the prophets, said, 'O my Lord, I have never been eloquent, neither in the past nor even now, but I am slow of speech and slow of tongue. O my Lord, please send someone else.'

"And it's not likely your grandmother would be willing to give such testimony even if she hadn't lost her memory. She and your aunt Millicent have funny ideas about being fired up over things like religion and the bible, about how it's not proper and how it's poor breeding to discuss religion.

"They were brought up by your great-grandfather, Jonathan Kingsford, to treat religion with a 'kindly countenance.' As he used to say, 'the intellectually and culturally deprived require it to give them a reason for their sad existence.' I wonder what the old blue-blood had to say when he met God face to face. I'll bet he lost his composure then."

Jeremiah Bowman snorted, and he felt a bit warmer as angry recollections of his father-in-law grew fresh in his mind. He tried to control his anger which he knew was his greatest flaw, but thoughts of his father-in-law's blue blood always made his own blood boil red.

Like the apostle Paul, old Jonathan was the sting in his flesh to keep him humble. Jonathan had been a snob and had raised his daughters with an exaggerated sense of their own status. He wanted his daughters to assume even a more superior posture than he had, and sometimes Jeremiah thought the old man had been successful.

"Do you know what 'proper' means, Naomi?"

"Like being dressed up?" she asked.

"Something like that," he said. "It's like sitting down

to eat with white gloves on your hands. It's a clumsy way to eat, but you never get your hands dirty, and when the meal's all done, your hands are just as soft and fine as before you started.

"Your great-grandfather Jonathan Kingsford was that way. The first time I met him, when I was allowed to go into his house," he recalled, still angry at the memory after fifty-two years and angry with himself for being angry, "he had on a tuxedo with a high, stiffed white collar and a black bow tie, and he shook my hand with his gloves on like I had just finished pitching cow pies.

"He was a mannered man, Naomi, tall and neat and groomed like a cock in a hen coop, but I never did get to like him. If he disdained me because I was bad or even because I was poor, I'd have understood him not wanting to give me your Grandma for a wife. It wasn't for any of those reasons though. It was because I just didn't have the right social standing, the right pedigree like some kind of pure bred animal."

The years hadn't softened his memories of the old man, he thought with sadness, ashamed of his sin, that he didn't have the grace to forgive Jonathan. Before he died, he had to summon up all his resources, and with the Lord's help, convince himself that Jonathan wasn't to blame because he hadn't known what he was doing to his daughters.

"You married Grandma though," Naomi said. "So you won?" she said cheerfully. "You won Grandma and beat great-grandfather."

"I did," he said. "I did win, didn't I?" But he knew it wasn't true. Sarah got her way with her own determination.

"Now you listen to me, Naomi," he said, "we have to plan our strategy, but I think the two miracles should provide us with the three votes we need."

As they walked a bit farther, they saw a crowd outside the building where the supervisors were going to meet.

People in the township were passionate about politics, and they were afraid if they didn't attend, the supervisors might try to pull something over on them. They voted for them, but they didn't trust them.

A few acquaintances greeted Naomi and Jonathan as they went into the building, but there were still hard feelings toward Jeremiah because they thought he had the power to cure, but wouldn't cure again because of what they had done to him at Carroll's wake and to Naomi on Palm Sunday.

Mr. Sanders looked at Naomi and was about ready to tell her the room would be filled with adult voters, but then he changed his mind and let her go in. He decided there would be room for everyone.

The three supervisors were seated when Naomi and Jeremiah entered the room. They were on an elevated platform, sitting in back of a large desk, and there was a microphone at each seat. There was a podium at which each speaker stood, facing the audience, and there was also a microphone at the podium. There was room for about two hundred people to sit down, and the place was almost full.

"As you know," Peter McNally began, "when we receive requests to speak at the meeting, we choose lots to determine the order in which each township member speaks. The problem tonight is that there are twelve people who want to speak, and so we must limit the time to three minutes each."

There was a murmur of unrest, but with twelve people and the regular business meeting after they were finished, no one wanted to be there until midnight.

As secretary of the Board, John Healey had the paper with the order of speakers. "Mr. Bowman will speak first. You have three minutes from the time you get to the podium."

Jeremiah rose and stood up as straight as he could. "I wanted my grand-daughter, Naomi, to bear testimony to my words, but there's not enough time, and I reckon many of you have seen what I've done anyway, not on my own power, but through the grace and power of God."

"We're not looking for a sermon tonight," Peter O'Malley said, a hint of sarcasm in his tone. "You have only three minutes."

John Healey was upset, but very formal. "The rules say we have to add one minute to his time for any interruption by a supervisor. Go ahead, Mr. Bowman." Healey loved order, and he hated to lose control so early in the evening.

"Since you give me such a short time, I'll be brief. I ask the township supervisors to erect an alabaster statue, a fair likeness of me, in the town square, and on the base where the statue will stand, to carve:

>'In memory of Jeremiah Bowman,
>declared a saint of God by this
>township, in recognition
>of the miracles he has wrought, and
>the acts of love he has done for as
>many as he was able. We declare his
>life an example for all to imitate."

Before Jeremiah sat down, he walked over to John Healey and gave him a copy of the words to inscribe on the statue.

No one, Catholic or Protestant, doubted the miracles. There were too many witnesses for doubting. And everyone knew of his charity, seeking out those who were bereft to help them.

On the other hand, no one in the audience, even the Protestants, could believe what he had said, what he had asked for. The Protestants were humiliated that one of their own should ask for a statue of himself placed in the town square to be adored like Catholics adored their so-called "saintly" idols.

The Catholics were wounded that any Protestant would intrude on one of their sacred customs, in which their spiritual leader canonized people, raising them to sainthood in a religious ceremony presided over by the pope himself. It seemed as if their holy beliefs were being trampled on and usurped by this madman.

A loud murmuring of protest ran through the room, and Ned Oates was afraid it would escalate into chaos, and perhaps even violence. Jeremiah sat in his seat, unperturbed by the anger swelling about him, lost in a prayer of gratitude that God had given him the strength to carry out his command by asking the supervisors to fulfill the will of the Lord. What would happen was out of his hands. He was the messenger, the vessel of clay, not the Lord of heaven and earth, not the one through whom came the power, and to whom belonged the glory.

As the noise grew louder and more strident, Ned Oates pounded on the gavel at his desk, shouting "order" until the crowd settled down. They respected Oates because he was the most balanced and fair of the three supervisors.

"Jeremiah," Oates said, "please stand up where you are, and you, Naomi, if your grandfather needs support." They both stood, and Naomi put her arm around her grandfather in case he began to feel weak after the ordeal.

"Jeremiah, all of us here are aware of the two miracles you performed. None of us can say they weren't miracles, because there is medical testimony that both of the people were dead and are now alive. I must say, however, that most of us are bewildered by how they happened and why they happened.

"As a community, we're also aware of how many wonderful things you've done for the poor even to the point of giving up your own clothing and money when they were in dire need.

"The two other supervisors and I will take your request under consideration, but I must tell you I don't think there is any chance of doing what you requested. We represent the township, the legal system, the governing body. This great country of ours has always maintained a separation between church and state, between religious and civil affairs. I know I'm not as learned as you in the scriptures, Jeremiah, but even Christ said, 'render to Caesar what belongs to Caesar, and to God, what belongs to God.'

"And so I'm afraid that for the good of all the citizens, we must uphold that separation. If you want to ask the Baptist church to erect a statue in honor of the wondrous deeds you have done through the power of the Lord, that's fine. But you can't expect a civil body to get involved in religion."

Jeremiah looked at Mr. Oates. "Thank you, sir, for your kindness and consideration. What I asked was what the Lord commanded me to ask, and He will decide how His will is done. Let's go home, Naomi. I'm very tired."

Naomi helped her grandfather out of the chair, and he put his arm around her. "I don't feel well, Naomi," Jeremiah said, loud enough to be heard by some at the meeting. "Perhaps we can get someone to give us a ride home."

"I'll take you home," Bill Carroll said.

"You'll do no such thing," Mary said, tugging at his pants. "You just sit down right where you are."

"Let go of me, woman. I owe Jeremiah my life. The least I can do is take him home when he's not feeling well."

Mary felt embarrassed and humiliated. It was the first time since their marriage that he didn't obey her. She would speak to him when they got home.

Bill took Jeremiah's other arm and helped Naomi bring him down the steps and put him into his car.

"Jeremiah, your breathing is labored. Maybe I should take you to the hospital."

"No. No. I have to go home to Sarah." Jeremiah was agitated, and Bill was afraid to insist he go to the hospital.

"I'll open your window, Jeremiah. Maybe some fresh

air will help you. It was stuffy in there."

"You're probably right, Bill. I'll be O.K. once we get going. Talking in front of the supervisors was more of a strain than I thought it would be."

Bill started the motor and moved forward slowly. "Well, if there was a way to vote for what you proposed, I'd vote for it. There's no natural explanation for what you did for me. It was a miracle, all right."

"Well, as I said over and over, it was the Lord working through me, not me. If I had the power on my own to do such things, I'd make myself feel an awful lot better right now."

"You'll be all right when we get you home, Grandpa. Now that you've done and said what the Lord wanted, you can take a good, long rest."

As they pulled in the driveway, Anna came out to meet them. She had been sitting with Sarah, but she was nervous about Jeremiah going to the township meeting and had been anxious for them to return. When she heard the car pull in, she was hoping nothing had gone wrong.

Naomi and Bill brought Jeremiah into the house and sat him in his chair.

"Naomi, get Millicent and Matthew," Anna said. "The lights are on in their house. They must be home. Quick."

"I better leave," Bill said. "The meeting will be almost over, and my wife will be waiting for me. Goodbye, Jeremiah. I hope you're feeling better."

"Goodbye, Bill," Jeremiah said, "and thank you."

"Dad, we have to get you to the hospital. I'm going to call for an ambulance," Anna said. "You must be having some kind of heart problem."

"No, don't, Anna. My time has come. The Lord told me. Help me up. I want to sit next to your mother."

Sarah was sitting on the couch, watching everything that was going on, but not understanding. She took one of the pillows from the couch and put it over her stomach. It made her feel better as she clutched it to herself.

As Jeremiah pushed himself out of the chair with one hand, Anna put her hand under his armpit and helped him stand. His lungs were gurgling as he moved toward Sarah. He turned around, and Anna helped him sit down.

"I'm leaving you Sarah," Jeremiah said, as he took her hand, "but I want you to know that when I meet the angels, and they ask me what was the greatest thing that happened to me in my life, I'm going to tell them it was loving you."

Some neurological connector made a synapse for a moment, and Sarah smiled, leaning her head on Jeremiah's shoulder.

Millicent and Matthew came in.

Matthew went over to Jeremiah, and knelt down in front of him on one knee. "A little too much exertion for one night, I expect."

"A little bit," Jeremiah said.

"You'll be fine," Matthew said, knowing he wouldn't. "We both have long lives in front of us." Matthew stood up and put his arm around Millicent.

Naomi sat down on the other side of her grandfather on the couch. Her grandfather put his other arm around her, smiled at Anna, and murmured to himself, 'I forgive Jonathan Kingsford.' Then he slipped into the arms of the Lord.

Yahweh: The Finale

Naomi told Matthew Arnold that the township supervisors had refused to erect a statue in honor of her grandfather and declare him a saint despite the miracles he had performed and the good deeds he had done.

Matthew believed in no God, no miracles, no afterlife, no saints, no prayer, no world of transcendence. But he was an iconoclast. As a student, as a professor, as a citizen, he had believed the majority were in the wrong. He honored the individual, and looked down on the crowd. Like Plato, he believed in the rule of the philosopher-king, of the highly intelligent ruling the herd. He thought of himself as a philosopher-king.

Years ago while visiting his parents in Carbon, he had purchased an acre of land adjacent to the town square, thinking he might make a profit if the town of Carbon decided to expand outwards, but it never did.

Matthew had come to consider Jeremiah one of the most unique individuals he had ever known. He thought of him as a religious fanatic, but one who lived the truth of all he preached.

And so, he decided to make the land a shrine in honor of Jeremiah. He had made a good sum of money when interest rates and Certificate of Deposits went skyward during the presidency of Jimmy Carter. He used a small part of it to pay one of his sculptor friends from his teaching days who was now retired to carve an alabaster statue of Jeremiah, and inscribe these words at its base:

> In memory of the first Protestant saint,
> Jeremiah Bowman,
> miracle worker and minister
> to all in need

Millicent, Matthew, Naomi and Anna did the landscaping and tended to its upkeep. People came and prayed to Jeremiah, and those who believed were made whole.

Jeremiah has been a big help in solving some of my problems up here. First he persuaded Francis of Assisi to bunk with the Birdman of Alcatraz, and he talked me into giving them a few birds if they promised to keep the birds inside and not let them fly around.

He helped John the Baptist build his first franchise location, and even tasted a few locusts. He told John he thought a little mustard mixed with the honey might make them more tasty, but John didn't think much of that idea. He wanted them to taste like locusts.

Somewhere Jeremiah got a copy of both the *Iliad* and the *Odyssey*, and he asked Jerome if he could translate them into English for him. He told Jerome he'd help him copyright the translation, and maybe he'd make a lot of money in royalties. That should keep Jerome out of my way for a good twenty years.

His latest project is trying to fix the Little Flower up with Augustine. If he pulls that off, he'll be the number one miracle worker up here.

Bill Carroll came up last week, and he seems happy enough. Being raised from the dead doesn't last forever.

And next month Sarah will arrive. I still have my money on Jeremiah.

Well, that's the end of my novel. My editor says it needs some polishing. After that, we'll submit it for publication. Please buy it, and make it a best seller.

The alpha and the omega